ROYAL SALVATION

SHADOW ELITE BOOK 3

MADDIE WADE

Royal Salvation
Shadow Elite Book Three
By Maddie Wade

Published by Maddie Wade
Copyright © May 2022

Cover: Clem Parsons-Metatec
Editing: Black Opal Editing
Formatting: Black Opal Editing

Acknowledgments

I am so lucky to have such an amazing team around me without which I could never bring my books to life. I am so grateful to have you in my life, you are more than friends you are so essential to my life.

My wonderful beta team, Greta, and Deanna who are brutally honest and beautifully kind. If it is rubbish you tell me, it is and if you love it you are effusive. Your support means so much to me.

My editor—Linda at Black Opal Editing, who is so patient. She is so much more than an editor, she is a teacher and a friend.

Thank you to my group Maddie's Minxes, your support and love for Fortis, Eidolon, Ryoshi and now Shadow Elite you are so important to me. Special thanks to Rowena, Tracey, Faith, Rachel, Carolyn, Kellie, Maria, Rochelle, Becky, Vicky, Greta, Deanna, Sharon and Linda L for making the group such a friendly place to be.

My UK PA Clem Parsons who listens to all my ramblings and helps me every single day.

My ARC Team for not keeping me on edge too long while I wait for feedback.

Lastly and most importantly thank you to my readers who have embraced my books so wholeheartedly and shown a love for the stories in my head. To hear you say that you see my characters as family makes me so humble and proud. I hope you enjoy Justice and Lucía's love story as much as I did.

Cover: Clem Parsons @Metatec
Editing: Black Opal Editing

To those of you that leave reviews, post your love of social media and generally support authors, thank you. You will never know how much your support means to me.

PROLOGUE

His heart racing, Justice Carson, aka Reaper, ducked his head inside the barren home of one of the elders of the village. For days, he and his men had been in search of the leader of the Islamist Extremist Group known as the Islamic Emirate. The leader, Abdul Omar, was meant to be hiding out in the village that was nestled in the Hindu Kush region close to the Salang Tunnel. The Salang Tunnel linked Northern Afghanistan and the Parwan Provence and was a crucial point of conflict in the war between the groups.

A muffled scream tore through the dirt walls of the deserted home and he raised his weapon. He and his men, of the Australian SAS's Charlie Squadron, were leading this mission. As the detonation specialist and bomb expert, it was his job to make sure they didn't find any of the IEDs that were scattered around the mountain like sprinkles on a kid's birthday cake.

Moving through the dark space, the cool air of the coming night bit into his skin, even through the thick military-grade clothing he wore and the Bergen on his back heavy with supplies.

Seeing nothing, he moved through the village, nodding to his teammate Joker, who was across the sand path that separated the village down the centre. This was a six-man team, himself, Joker, Denny, Monk, Chess, and Playboy. The latter was a man he couldn't stand and only tolerated for the sake of the team, and because of who his father was.

Playboy was just that, a man who thought he was a gift to women and thought that every female should fall at his feet. He was arrogant, cocky, and a fucking danger to others, but his commanding officer wouldn't hear of it.

He was a good enough soldier, but not good enough for this team. He and everyone else knew it, but he was protected in a way he never should have been, and it would cost someone their life one day.

As Joker and Denny ducked into the home across the way, an eerie feeling of dread worked its way up Reaper's spine. It was something he'd learned to listen to from a young age. As a boy, he and his younger brother Caleb had known that if you got that feeling it meant their father a—well-respected Officer in the Australian Military—was in one of his moods.

As the oldest, Reaper had always protected his brother, who couldn't take the hits he could.

It had made him a man, or that at least that was the mantra his father spouted to justify the abuse he meted out to his oldest son. In some ways, that was true because Reaper could just about take any beating he was given and not flinch. It was how he'd got his name. His friends said he was so close to the grim reaper on a few occasions in his career that he was probably him wearing Justice Carson's skin.

The sound came again, a muffled scream but louder than before, and he motioned for Monk to go around the other side, and they'd converge on whatever or whoever it might be. The formation of three two-man teams worked well for them, and he knew Playboy and Chess would've cleared the area already, but he couldn't get the bad feeling out of his head.

As he slid his body along the wall of the hut, he angled his weapon so he wouldn't be caught off guard. It was a vow he'd made the day he'd stood up to his father and told him if he ever touched either one of them again, he'd put him in the grave. Far from being angry, his father had seemed proud, the crazy fucker believing he'd made him a man.

Rounding the corner, he stopped for a second, not sure what he was seeing until the horrific scene in front of him became clear.

Playboy had his pants around his knees and had a woman, no, a girl of no more than sixteen, pressed against the cold wall of the hut raping her. Chess, who he'd believed to be a good man, was laughing as he made lewd jokes about her as she cried and struggled to get free.

Reaper struggled to understand what was happening. They were looking for a damn terror cell and two of his men were raping a young Afghan girl and laughing about it.

Filled with sudden rage, a red mist falling over everything, he launched himself at Playboy. The shock on his face would've almost been comical if the disgust Reaper felt about his crime hadn't been so visceral.

His fist landed in the other man's face, and he felt the bone crunch underneath his blow. He beat him until his arms gave way and someone pulled him free from the silent man whose screams had died down.

Reaper looked up and saw Joker and Monk detaining Chess. Turning, he saw Denny was the one who'd pulled him off Playboy, who was alive but badly beaten. As far as Reaper was concerned, he was lucky he hadn't killed him but he believed in the justice system and would drag his ass home so he could face charges of rape.

Seeing the wide-eyed look of the girl cowering on the ground, he moved towards her. She shrunk back, terror in her eyes. Reaper held out his hand, only wanting to check she was okay but knowing how frightened she must be amongst these foreign men who'd invaded her peace and attacked her and each other. "It's okay, I just want to make sure you're okay."

Reaper knew she had no idea what he was saying but he hoped

his voice conveyed that he wasn't a threat, when, of course, he was. All the soldiers there were a threat in some way, whether they wanted to be or not and no matter their intentions.

He tried asking if she was okay again and she nodded. He moved closer, knowing that Joker and Monk had his back. Those were two men he wasn't wrong about. Her startling blue eyes and blonde hair beneath the robes she wore were surprising in this region but not unheard of.

He couldn't help but stare but dragged his eyes away from the child back to Joker. "Find out if anyone in this village knows who she is."

Backing away, he removed a blanket from his Bergen and offered it to her, which she took, as her body curled into itself. He could hardly look at her without feeling a blood-boiling rage for the piece of filth who was unconscious on the cool sand. He'd made more work for them by doing what he had. They'd likely have to carry Playboy out of there now. Although a big part of him wanted to leave the animal here to die from his injuries, he knew he wouldn't do that.

When he looked back, the girl was gone. He and his men spent an hour looking for her, moving in and out of the properties, avoiding the glances of the women who kept their eyes averted. The men, although they weren't warriors, looked ready to kill to defend the people from the soldiers who, up until that night, they'd been helping.

Gathering their gear, they headed out to the landing zone where they'd exfil and report back to base. The trek was long but uneventful, only made difficult by Playboy who was moaning now in pain.

"Shut the fuck up, you pervert, before I really give you something to cry about."

"Come on, boss, it was just a bit of fun."

Reaper's cool gaze cut to Chess, who was watching him as if he was overreacting about a food order being wrong, not the attack on a young girl.

In the back of the helo, Reaper launched himself across the seat and grabbed Chess by the throat. "Bowling is fun, football is fun. Raping an innocent girl isn't fun. It's a crime, you mother fucker."

Chess was turning blue, but Reaper didn't care. He wanted the man to understand but with sudden clarity, he knew he never would. Any man who had to be told that what they'd done was wrong would never see the act for the vile, disgusting thing it was.

Letting him go, he stayed silent on the flight back. Playboy was stretchered away as soon as they hit the ground and he and his team were separated. Sitting in his dirty, filth-ridden clothes, he thought about the girl and prayed to a God he wasn't sure was listening that she'd recover.

His commanding officer ushered him inside the room and closed the door. Twenty-four hours later, his illustrious career with the Australian Special Forces was over. His CO had been sympathetic, but Playboy was the son of a high-ranking general and thus protected.

Reaper had thought he'd be prosecuted, that he'd get his just desserts, but he was being sent home to recover before he was returned to the very role that Reaper was being stripped of. His team had come to see him as he packed his gear, the picture of him and his brother the only personal item he had.

They'd told him how Chess had said his words were lies and despite their testimony, the brass had believed Chess and Playboy.

Two weeks later he was in a bar in his hometown of Cairns, where his mother was from and still lived since she'd divorced his asshole of a father, nursing a ten-year malt at eleven am in the morning.

Tossing back the fiery liquid he slammed the glass down and motioned for the bartender to bring him another. As he contemplated his life and the screw up it had become, he wondered what he'd do now. Perhaps he could stay with Caleb and his husband John for a while.

They lived on the Gold Coast and were both successful architects with a beachfront home. Caleb had reached out when he'd heard what happened from their mother, but he hadn't been able to face anyone yet.

A presence beside him made him look left to see a man with dark hair and wide shoulders take the seat beside him. Reaper wasn't in the mood for talking. He recognised a fellow operator when he saw one and had no intention of being friendly.

The man ordered a drink and sat quietly sipping the liquid for a good half an hour before Reaper'd had enough. Turning, he glanced at him through bleary eyes and wondered when the last time he'd been truly sober was. "Do I know you?"

The man paused with his drink halfway to his mouth and looked at him. "Nope."

"Then what the hell do you want?"

"I just want to know if you're finished wallowing in self-pity yet or if you need a few more days to pull your head from your ass."

Reaper heard the British accent and frowned before he realised the insult the man had thrown down. Standing, Reaper swayed. He'd obviously drunk more than he thought. "What the fuck did you say to me?"

The man ignored him and ordered two coffees from the bartender.

"You don't fucking know me."

"Don't I? Justice Carson aka Reaper. You have a brother Caleb, who is married to John. They're currently trying to adopt a child. Your mum lives a quiet life in Cairns working for a local law firm as a personal assistant. Your dad is Colonel Malcolm Carson and is a complete hardass."

The man stood and he was a smidge taller than Reaper's six foot two inches and slightly broader but also a few years older. A flicker of memory lingered in his brain but was gone before he could hold on to it.

"Let's get a seat and you can decide if you want to come work for me."

Feeling suddenly sober, Reaper followed the man to a corner seat with a table and took the chair facing the door as the other man angled his chair to do the same. "Who are you?"

"My name is Jack Granger and I run a private security company."

Reaper moved to stand. "Not interested."

"That's fine, but if you walk away, you'll never have the chance to get your revenge on Playboy for what happened in the Hindu Kush."

Reaper snarled, his lip curling in open hostility as he grabbed for the man's throat.

As fast as he made contact, he was laid flat on his ass, the other man standing over him with a deadly glare. "You ever lay hands on me again, I'll fucking bury you where you stand. Do I make myself clear?"

Still reeling from the quickest takedown he'd ever seen, Reaper got on his feet, a grudging admiration forming in his gut. Rubbing the wrist where Jack had twisted it with such speed to put him on his ass, he sat opposite and watched in silence as their coffee was delivered.

"Everything good here, mates?"

"Yep, all good," Reaper responded, his interest piqued now. What did this stranger know about Playboy and what happened, and why was he there? Taking a sip of the hot brew he felt himself sobering up fast, caffeine and adrenaline would do that to a guy. "How do you know what happened?"

"I told you, I know a lot of things. What I want to know is if you're ready to walk away from this life and begin a new one."

"Meaning?"

"Fuck, you talk less than I do. I mean, I work for someone who needs people with a good moral compass and who are willing to get their hands dirty to defend those who can't defend themselves."

"So, a job?"

"No, this isn't a job, it's a life. Your life and existence will be

7

wiped from any database, and you'll cease to exist. Your family will think you work for a mountain rescue company in Wales, but in truth, you'll be doing the jobs governments are too weak to sanction and saving the very people those governments promise to protect."

"Illegal black ops?"

"Black Ops, yes. Illegal, not exactly. We're under the highest authority, but no government or agency will know we exist. You'll sign an agreement, which if broken, won't end with you going to jail. It will end with you in a box six-foot underground."

Reaper should be getting up and walking away but he was intrigued. "Can I think about it?"

"No, when I leave this place so does the offer. You'll wake up tomorrow and there will be no evidence we even spoke."

"How does it benefit me?"

Jack smiled but it held no humour. "Simple, you get revenge on Playboy and Chess. You also get to make sure men like them are no longer protected."

Everyone had always thought he'd joined the army because of his dad, and in part that was true. But not because he respected the man everyone thought was a hero but because he hated him and wanted to prove who was better. When he'd begun the work though, he'd found helping people and protecting others was something he thrived on.

The night that child was hurt on his watch was the worst of his life, and he'd never forget the look on her face or the feeling of failure he'd had. "What happened to the girl they attacked?"

"She was killed by her family later that night. The shame she'd brought to them was too much and they killed her."

Reaper breathed through his nose at the blunt words, his head spinning in a thousand different directions. He'd known it was possible, but he couldn't take her with them, not when two of the six men had been the ones to attack her. "And Playboy?"

"He's back in the field in your old job as team leader."

"Did the others sell me out?"

Jack shook his head. "No. They fought for you, but Playboy is the son of a powerful man. You were never going to win that fight. But I promise if you join us, you'll get your chance to right this wrong."

"Where do I sign?"

Jack stood, throwing some bills on the table and began to walk away, before stopping and looking back. "Well, are you coming?"

"What? I leave now?"

"You best know those credit cards you have won't work. Justice Carson doesn't exist on paper any longer."

The bright light of the Australian sun hit him in the eyes as they emerged from inside the bar to find a black SUV waiting, the engine running. "You were that sure I'd agree?"

"Yes."

"How?" His hand rested on the closed door of the vehicle, and he got a good look at the man, recognising Jack Granger as the elite British SAS operator who'd been unceremoniously removed from the Military for unknown reasons.

"You remind me of me."

Reaper arched an eyebrow. "Not sure that's a compliment."

Jack's lips twitched and he had a feeling that was as much as he'd get.

"Pack warm. Wales will freeze your balls off after this heat."

"Can't wait."

"You never know, you might enjoy it."

That was the day Reaper's life took on new meaning and he never looked back.

CHAPTER 1

THE DRIVE DOWN FROM LONGTOWN TO LONDON HAD ONLY ONE BENEFIT AS far as he could see, and that was it gave him an excuse to stop in and see Snow and Fleur, along with the bonus of winding Sebastian up. With Snow splitting her time between Shadow HQ and her new home, Reaper knew it was only a matter of time before Sebastian had her barefoot and pregnant and locked down.

That would be the smartest move that asshole had ever made, after asking Snow to marry him and falling on his sword for her at least. The team was changing and his role in it, hence why he was on babysitting duty for a pampered Princess who thought it was fun to play war photographer for the next six months.

He glanced at the file he had on the passenger seat beside him and gritted his jaw. Princess Lucía Castille was second in line to the throne of Spain. Twenty-eight years old with a degree in photojournalism and political science, she was clearly smart enough. But putting her in the field was a risk to herself and anyone with her, and that was the part he didn't like.

This entitled woman was willing to risk every member of her team to have her way, with no thought for those around her. Now he was being drafted as a special favour for Jack and Queen Lydia no less, to be her bodyguard.

Bás had asked him weeks ago when the shit was still happening with Snow and her family and he'd refused. But when it ended, so had the idea that he had a choice. The fact the Princess was ridiculously beautiful only made his job harder. Even with her body and hair covered in the part of the country she was travelling to, she was still such a beauty it was hard to ignore.

Which was why, to his utter disgust, she was going to have a fake passport and identity while she did her thing, and he was the stupid schmuck who'd be playing her husband. Partly to ward off the advances of other men, but mostly so he could stay close enough to her to properly protect her, while still adhering to the laws and customs of the country they were visiting.

He still had to share that little titbit of information with the Princess as all their communications had been through email and had gone through Bás. But her father, the King of Spain, had approved it in a bid to give his youngest daughter what she wanted and keep her safe.

Bás had made it very clear he wasn't to touch Princess Lucía, and by that, he meant fuck her. Which he had no intention of doing. Spoiled little girls weren't his type, no matter how beautiful they were.

Reaper loved women of all kinds, always had and he respected them. Contrary to what it looked like to others, he didn't have an ex he didn't think of with fondness, even if sometimes their names alluded him. He gave respect and love but he never ever gave promises or commitment.

His life was one of free love. Women loved him, and he loved them, and everyone was happy when it ended after a very brief but satisfying spin through the sheets. His blond hair and blue eyes, along with his easy smile and square jaw, helped. Working with Shadow had honed his body into pure muscle. Not bulk, but lean, toned abs and chest and it sure helped him with the chicks.

Not that he paraded around shirtless like Hurricane. No, he used his humour and charm to get women into bed and it often didn't require any real effort on his part. Which was why Snow called him a heartbreaker, but she was wrong. He never broke hearts. He didn't have it in him to hurt a woman.

His mother had always said he had a soft side and it had driven his father crazy, almost making him crueller as if to thrust what he perceived as a weakness out of his psyche. Reaper was his mother's son and it had always been her he'd turned to for guidance. His brother had also followed their mother. He was kind, gentle, much more so than Reaper was, and it drove his father crazy.

A wave of longing for time with his family hit him and he vowed to call them as soon as he could. Caleb and John now had two children, a boy and a girl, a niece and nephew he hardly knew and that made him sad. He had pictures and sent gifts for every occasion, but it didn't make up for his lack of time spent with them.

Pulling off the motorway he turned towards Whitmore, Essex. He didn't know this area well, but he'd looked it up and it looked like a picture of an English village found on a chocolate box. Half-timber houses and thatched cottages lined the green, many dating back to the fourteenth century.

It was quaint but it was a disaster for someone like him who needed to slip in unseen and blend into the background. With an active Parish Council and an even more active neighbourhood watch, if the twitching curtains were anything to go by, this was going to be a shit show.

Why in God's name the Princess had chosen this place was anyone's guess. Apart from being pretty, it was a nightmare for a security specialist. He took the turn his SatNav was indicating and followed the narrow road, the hedgerow on either side full of life and berries. Stopping twice for an oncoming car, he pulled his Land Rover over as far as he could into the hedge, wincing each time as the thorns scratched the paintwork.

He wasn't precious about his cars, but he took care of them as he did all his things. If the dirty look the farmer was giving him was any indication, he didn't approve of what he obviously considered city folk. It had been something of a culture shock for him moving to a small village like Longtown, where strangers were often met with suspicion. It had taken some time and the help of the local landlord but eventually the people of Longtown had accepted the newcomers. Now they were as much a part of the furniture as the sheep, of which there were thousands.

Finally free of the narrow road, he made the turn into what he expected to be a large estate house but when he pulled up at the address he was given, it was to see a small cottage with one of the illustrious thatched rooves. Reaper internally groaned, wondering what in hell the Spanish security office were thinking letting the second in line to the throne live there.

The roof was a fire hazard, and the latches on the windows were barely functional against the wind, let alone against an intruder sent to harm her. Parking, he stepped out of the vehicle and looked around, taking in his surroundings. The more he looked, the more he noticed that his first assessment had been a little off.

Cameras covered the front of the property and he saw the blinking light of an alarm at least. The front door opened, and he was confronted with a vision he hadn't been expecting. Princess Lucía stood on the threshold in faded jeans and a white shirt tied at the waist, she had white pumps on her feet and her hair in a bun that was meant to look effortless but probably took hours to perfect.

"Well, are you going to stand and stare or are you coming inside?"

The rich, smooth velvety tone of her voice and the strong accent she spoke in, instantly made his trousers tight in the crotch. Snapping out of the shock, he stepped forward and she stepped back, letting him inside her home. The scent of her perfume, which wasn't the deep seductive tones he'd expected from her but a light lemony, vanilla fragrance, made him want to see if she tasted as sweet as she smelled and he instantly frowned.

When he was fully inside the house, he looked around the space. The front door opened directly into the living room, which was homey with a soft cream couch in front of a lit fire and colourful blankets were thrown over the back in a haphazard way. A glass of red wine was on the wooden coffee table next to a selection of editorials on photography and art.

The kitchen was to the right and held a small table piled high with books and camera equipment, clearly unused for what it was designed. A simple oven and hob with clean counter tops made of oak, the same as the flooring, and white units, made the space feel bigger than it was.

This complete change from what he was expecting threw him, making him irrationally annoyed when he was usually the chilled-out one. Walking around, he took in the room and then turned back to the Princess, who was watching him with caution and something that looked like familiarity but they'd never met. He'd certainly remember having met this woman before. "You usually let in strange men with no identification?"

Her brows rose and he saw her suck in a breath through her nose as if looking for divine patience. "No, but you're hardly a stranger. Bás sent me your picture and I knew you were here before you arrived, as I had four calls from people in the village warning me a stranger was headed this way."

"I see."

Lucía stepped forward and took the glass of wine off the table, holding it in front of her like it would keep her safe. "Would you like some food or wine?"

Reaper shook his head. "No. I ate before I arrived and I don't drink on the job."

"Fair enough. Your room is through the back and to the left of the bathroom. Food is in the fridge, help yourself. I have work to do."

Reaper was stunned silent for a second as she dismissed him like he was hired help, which to be fair he was, but the little Spanish

Princess needed to learn really quick that he was the one calling the shots here, not her.

As she stepped to her kitchen table, ignoring his presence, he knew he needed to set things straight right now or she'd be the type to run roughshod over him.

Moving silently, he placed his body right behind hers, his much bigger frame dwarfing her smaller, petite one. She wasn't short, probably five foot five and she had curves that he'd noticed despite trying not to, but next to him she was still small.

The temptation to run his tongue down the back of her neck and watch her shiver was almost too much, but he was there to keep her safe, not see if she felt and tasted as good as she looked.

"I think you have the wrong idea, Princess." He couldn't hide the sneer in his voice, as much from frustration as her attitude.

Lucía gasped as she turned, not having sensed him and she stumbled, her hands flying out to catch herself as her palms landed on his chest, his hand cupping her elbow to steady her.

"You shouldn't sneak up on people." Her admonishment would've been much more effective if her nipples hadn't been visible through the white shirt, hard and proud and calling to him.

"And you should be more aware of your surroundings. Isn't that what photographers do? See and notice things us mortals don't."

"Back up Mr...." She threw her hands up in the air, her Latin temper clearly visible. "What should I call you? I refuse to call you Reaper."

"Call me by my name. Justice."

He had no idea why he'd given her that. Nobody but his family called him that, but she was right, she could hardly call him Reaper in public if they were going to play husband and wife.

As soon as she said his name out loud as if trying it out for size, he knew it was a mistake. He liked the way it sounded on her tongue, the accent making it sound sensual.

"Then you must call me Lucía."

Reaper nodded. "We have a few things we need to discuss

regarding your security arrangements and the trip you have planned."

"Do we have to do it now?"

She looked past him as if looking for a way out and he suspected she thought such things were tedious and beneath her but that was tough shit.

"Yes, we do." His tone brooked no argument and he wondered if she'd fight him anyway and try and pull rank. In which case she'd find out quickly that when it came to her safety, he outranked her every time.

"Fine, let's get this over with."

She moved past him, her head held high, a regal baring about her which couldn't be ignored or faked. It wasn't forced, it was simply her. She was elegant and had class that couldn't be hidden, and he'd need to help her disguise that. Her whole being screamed money and privilege, and to some, that was a red flag waving 'come and get her'.

Taking a seat opposite her, he watched her lay her hands in her lap, her spine straight, as she waited for him to lay it out.

"First things first. When it comes to your safety, I'm in charge. If I say move, you move. If I say jump, you jump. You do not argue or hesitate. You do exactly as I say."

"Of course. I'm not an idiot, Justice, and this isn't my first time with a guard that wasn't part of the royal security team."

"Good. Another thing. I'll need a list of all your plans two days in advance if possible. If I decide something is too dangerous then it doesn't happen, no arguments. I'll have a tracker on your phone, and you'll be able to contact me twenty-four hours a day, every day. Where you go, I go."

"Well, that might become a little tricky in some places."

Justice tried to hide the grin that was creeping across his face as he saw the wariness on hers. "Not at all, after all, we're husband and wife!"

CHAPTER 2

"No!" Lucía got up from the sofa and paced to stand behind it, putting some space between her and the man who, after only twenty minutes, had her wanting to run for the hills. Never in her life had she reacted to a man on such a visceral level.

Tall and muscular with ocean blue eyes and a grin that promised mischief and pleasure in abundance, Justice was everything she shouldn't want and usually didn't find attractive. But if the way her nipples had woken up and the ache between her legs were anything to go by, then there was a new type in her inventory. Except this one was strictly off-limits. Not that most men weren't for her but at least she could look at most of them without guilt.

His announcement had thrown her for a loop. She could agree to the rest of his stipulations. She didn't like them, but she'd been surrounded by alpha males all her life and knew which battles to fight and which to concede, and the former was one to concede, but this—no way was she playing house with this man, even for a cover.

"Not an option. It's already been signed off by the King."

Lucía clenched her fist in an effort not to show her irritation. This sounded like something her father would do, although she was surprised he'd take it as far as a pretend husband. That required a certain level of intimacy, and her father was extremely protective of her. "Why wasn't I told or involved with this discussion?"

Justice shrugged. "No idea, Princess. Maybe speak to your father about that one."

Oh, she would be, first chance she got but until then, she needed some details. "How exactly would this work?"

"You and I will be given fake identities and a fake marriage licence. We'll live in the same house. When we travel, we'll stay in the same room. Separate beds of course but we'll need to make sure the maid service doesn't suspect anything. Where you go, so does your loving husband."

"I don't like this at all."

"Well then, pack up your cameras and do us all a favour and head home to the safety of the Palace."

Lucía was a little stunned at the hostility in his voice, but she was used to it. Nobody understood her passion for what she did. Even her father, who indulged her, believed it was something she needed to get out of her system before she settled down and started attending to her royal duties. Lucía had done everything in her power, to protect those she loved and continue being the person she was born to be, including working under the pseudonym Carla Cassidy and forgoing any credit for her work. All so she could capture the moments that mattered. "I get the feeling you don't like me, Justice."

He rolled his lip, frowning. "Not at all, I don't know you. I just think you're taking unnecessary risks with other people's lives just to get your own way."

"You think I'm a spoiled little rich girl playing games?"

"No, I think you're good at what you do, I've seen the pictures and you have talent, there aren't any games in that. But I do think you're being entitled by pushing this when you know the risks to you and every person who travels with you."

She did know the risks. Maybe he was right and she should give it up, but she had to go back to that village and see if the destruction she'd photographed had healed in any way. "Listen, I don't expect you to understand or even like me, but I can be professional if you can."

Years of training and watching her mother deal with difficult situations at her husband's side had left Lucía with all the tools she needed to get through this. However, her one sore spot or weak spot was her temper. She had a hot, quick temper that sometimes got her into trouble, and if anyone was going to push those buttons, she had a feeling it would be this man.

Good or not, something about him just irritated her in a way she couldn't explain. She was usually so calm and rational but since he'd walked in all she wanted to do was either fight with him or climb him like a tree.

"I can be professional, Princess."

"Lucía. My name is Lucía. Princess is just a title."

"Whatever you say."

Was he trying to get under her skin or was it just a simple clash of personalities? She didn't know but she was too tired to care, and she had a headache coming on from holding herself in check.

Perhaps she needed to put in a call to her father to see if she could get a new bodyguard, one that was less domineering and sexy, and more personable. "Is that all for tonight?"

"Yes."

He stood and she thought he might go to his car and bring a bag in, but he stepped close and her breath caught in her throat as his hand cupped her cheek, before caressing her chin and tipping her face up to his. It was against protocol to touch a member of the Royal family without an invitation to do so, and she hadn't given him that. Yet the tingle in her skin and the way her heart beat frantically in her chest, making her legs clench to ease the burning need between her thighs was a shock to her system.

This man pushed boundaries and ran over obstacles like a wrecking ball, and she'd have to be very careful not to get pulled into his magnetism. Thank goodness she didn't like him, or she'd be in big trouble.

Justice bent closer until she could see the twinkle of daring in his eyes and feel the soft mint of his breath on her face. He still held her chin, his touch soft and light, almost a caress. Her eyelids wanted to flutter closed and wait for the kiss she knew would come and would also knock her on her ass. The thought broke the spell and Lucía flinched away, worried she'd lean into his touch if she let him get away with this. "What are you doing?"

A sexy smirk, just the upturn of one side of his mouth, made her want to slap him and kiss him at the same time.

"Relax, angel, you gotta be comfortable being touched by your husband if you want us to sell this story."

He bent and kissed the corner of her mouth, and her eyes did close but before she could decide whether to enjoy it or punch his smug face, he was gone, the front door closing on his imposing back.

Humiliation and anger raced through her veins, and she didn't know whether to follow him outside and berate him for his insolent behaviour or retreat and hide in her room until she could get her thundering heart to calm down.

Deciding that option two was the best course of action, Lucía grabbed her phone and rushed into her bedroom, closing the door just as the front door opened and closed. Standing with her back against the door, she took a breath and blew it out slowly. This was just another obstacle in her way, and she'd find a way around or through it like she did every other.

Justice was simply something she had to overcome to achieve her goal. Going to her window, she glanced out at the garden she'd spent the summer tending. This place gave her a sense of eternal peace, living a life she loved. Whitmore had been an accidental find a few years ago and was now her haven when she needed to get away from her life as the second in line to the Spanish throne.

Her sister Maria was the heir apparent and had been groomed for the role her entire life. When the time came, God forbid not for many years, but when it did, Lucía would step up and become the support and confidant her sister needed.

Taking the cream easy chair and curling her legs underneath her, she dialled her father's personal cell. He answered with a smile in his voice as he always did for her. She was a daddy's girl through and through and they were a close family.

"Mi hija, it's wonderful to hear from you."

"Hi, Daddy," she said slipping into her native tongue.

"I miss you. When are you coming home?"

It was the same thing he always asked, and she knew it was only partly in jest. He loved her and wanted the best for her. They just didn't always see eye to eye on what that was, but he supported her and having a bodyguard was the compromise.

"That's actually why I called. This guard won't work for me."

Her father's tone lost the gentleness and became wary and over-protective. "Why? What did he do?"

How on earth did she explain to him that Justice was too attractive, too much male, and the thought of pretending to be his fake wife for the sake of her safety felt like an oxymoron. He was more dangerous than anything she'd faced before, but how could she explain that to her father without saying he made her lady parts tingle? "He's bossy and rude."

Her father's laughter came down the line, reminding her of all the times she'd laughed with him over simple things through the years.

"Ah, mi hija, it's his job to be bossy when it comes to your safety and men like him, who are the very elite at what they do, tend to be a little rough around the edges."

"But you expect me to pretend we're married."

"It's the only way you can go into the Muslim countries and have him close enough to keep you safe while still adhering to the customs and beliefs of the people. I do not need to tell you that the last thing we need is an international incident involving the Princess of Spain."

"But...."

"It's done, and he's a direct recommendation from Queen Lydia. It would be an insult to my cousin if we were to snub this man now."

Lucía knew she was caught, and her only action was to concede. "I understand."

"Listen, we have the annual autumn ball next week. Why don't you come, and we can meet this man? If he's unacceptable, I'll make new arrangements."

Her father was good. She either went to the ball where she knew her ex-boyfriend would be with his new Contessa, or she was stuck with Justice. Either option sounded awful right now. "I'm not sure. Let me speak with him and I'll let you know."

"As you wish, Lucía. Now, tell me about your village."

Her father loved hearing stories about the village and the people who'd taken her into their hearts and protected her as one of their own. She spent a few minutes talking to him about her friends before she hung up.

As she readied for bed, she listened to the noises in the room opposite as Justice moved around. He was quiet but it was comforting to have someone in the house with her. Loneliness shouldn't be something she suffered, especially having so many people at her beck and call. Yet so many nights she'd felt the deep ache of it as she fell asleep.

Tonight, as she closed her eyes, there was only the ghost feeling of his lips on the corner of her mouth.

CHAPTER 3

"Yes, Bás, I understand. I'll be on my best behaviour."

"Make sure you are. I don't want to have to come down there and kick your ass."

"Ass kicking isn't necessary. I'll be a perfect gentleman."

Reaper hung up and tossed the phone on the bed with a sigh. The Princess had gone running to daddy, who in turn had called Bás and chewed him out personally. He'd known he was crossing any number of boundaries with Lucía when he'd almost kissed her but something about her ground on his nerves. She wasn't what he'd expected, and Reaper didn't like surprises.

Having been up since five, he'd already showered, dressed, and checked the security measures on the property and the surrounding area. It was sufficient but not good enough. He was going to have more measures put in place later today, but first, he needed to apologise to his fake wife.

Leaving his room, he couldn't hear her moving around in the bedroom opposite as he had the previous night, the proximity of their rooms was both a blessing and curse. He was at least close enough to hear any sounds of distress but that also meant his mind had gone in some totally inappropriate directions. After the warning from Bás, he knew he had to shut that down and act like a professional.

Stepping into the open plan space, his eyes zeroed in on Lucía, who once again had her dark hair up off her face, showcasing the elegance of her neck as she bent over a laptop, a piece of toast hanging out of her mouth as she typed. The smell of coffee drew him into the kitchen as she turned, taking the toast from her mouth, and smiling.

"Good morning, Justice. Did you sleep well?"

He looked for sarcasm in her tone but didn't detect any. "I slept okay. You?"

"As well as I ever do."

Reaper poured himself a mug of coffee and lifted the pot to offer her some, but she declined with a shake of her pretty head.

"You don't sleep well?" He knew he shouldn't ask. It wasn't his job to get to know her. His job was to protect her but, in a way, the more he knew the easier that was.

"Not really. My mind is always too busy."

Reaper had a few suggestions on how he could help her relax but none were appropriate, so he kept his mouth shut. Sitting at a right angle to her at the table, he saw her pulse kick up in her neck and smiled into his mug. She was affected by him, and he liked that she was. He didn't want to be the only one battling this attraction and battle it he would. Bás had been clear, if he touched her, he was a dead man walking, and he knew Bás meant every word.

"Lucía, I'd like to apologise for yesterday. I was out of line behaving the way I did and I never should have laid a finger on you. It won't happen again. You have my word."

"Thank you and I think yesterday was a little trying for both of us. So why don't we start again?"

"I'd like that."

Lucía smiled at him, and it was like the sun coming out on a grey winter's day. She lit up and it made something ache in his chest to see it again. "I'm sure you know the plan for your security cover will stay in place, but I'll do everything I can to make sure it doesn't impact your life more than necessary."

He saw a blush tinge Lucía's cheeks and fought a groan.

"Thank you, I appreciate that."

"Now, tell me a bit more about this week's schedule. I have the long term one but as we don't fly out for a month, it would be good to know what the next few weeks have in store so I can make arrangements."

"Well, this week I have a few errands to run in the village and I promised to take some promotional shots for the Parish magazine. Next week my father has asked that I attend the Autumnal Ball. He'd like to meet you, and, in all honesty, I think it was his excuse to push me into coming."

Reaper tipped his head, watching her facial expressions as she spoke. She was very expressive and wore her feelings on her face. "You don't want to go?"

"It's not that I don't want to go. I want to see my family of course but meeting hundreds of people and being on all the time isn't my thing. I'm more for the background jobs, the charities, the good causes, that kind of thing."

"Well, I can understand that. What charities are you involved with?" He knew these little titbits of information would reveal way more about who she was as a person than any probing he might do.

Lucía's face lit up and once again he found himself wanting to freeze time so he could bask in her smile.

"I'm patron to the Books for All Foundation. It's a charity which collects and distributes books for children and helps them with reading. Many poorer families don't have the money for books and it's so important for kids to read."

"I agree. I love to read when I have time. That love comes from my mother and her taking the time to find a book I'd love."

"Exactly. It's not just about buying a book, it's about giving them a new world to escape the sometimes-awful conditions."

"What else?"

As Lucía listed off the charities she was involved with, Reaper got a better idea of who she was. Children's charities featured heavily, as did help for refugees. But she wasn't just a figurehead, she was involved with the planning and the implementation. She was a true humanitarian.

He wanted to ask her more about her life and work, but he didn't want to push his luck. "So, what's on today's agenda?"

"Well, I need to go into town and post a few letters and visit Mrs Howard and walk her dog. She had a fall a few weeks ago and until she's back on her feet we have a roster set up to walk Percy. You don't need to come with me though. My guard usually waits here when I go into the village."

Reaper frowned, trying not to overreact and ruin the peace between them after a rocky start, but he'd make sure that guard never worked doing close protection again. "Well, I'm not him and I'll be with you. When we meet with the villagers you'll need to tell them I'm your fiancé. That way if any pictures of us together are seen while we're in the Middle East, our cover is still in place."

"You really think that's necessary?"

"Absolutely."

Her eyebrows rose as she slipped from the table and made her way to the kitchen, her alluring scent tickling his nose. "How will I explain my sudden engagement?"

Reaper rose to follow her, tipping the dregs of his coffee in the sink before rinsing the mug and setting it in the dishwasher beside her plate and mug. "Tell them that I work overseas. Australia would be a good choice given my accent and that we recently reunited after a whirlwind romance. Does everyone know who you really are?"

Lucía nodded, her hand resting on the kitchen counter, her hip kicked out making her curves even more pronounced and enticing.

"Tell them the King asked you to keep it quiet and it's still a secret. Can you trust these people?"

"Absolutely. They've shown me nothing but kindness since I

bought this place, and they protect my privacy passionately. I'm one of them and this village is tight-knit. Once you're accepted here you become a part of something."

Reaper didn't analyse that, leaving it for later but he had a feeling it told him more about Lucía. Every word she spoke revealed something to him. "Then ask them to keep it quiet."

"Okay, I can do that."

"Good girl."

He saw her cheeks pink at his praise and had to turn away so his hard-on wouldn't be obvious. What was it about this woman that made him want to fuck her six ways from Sunday and never let go? He put it down to the fact she was out of bounds. The unattainable was always more desirable. "Now, last thing. The letters need to be posted from a few towns over. The postmark gives your location away to anyone who might intercept them."

"That seems a little paranoid."

"Maybe but I'd rather be paranoid than deal with the consequences. I can send them to my team in a big envelope and have them post them from their location. That would certainly throw anyone off the scent."

"Fine, whatever. As long as Mr and Mrs Jonson still get the money through their shop. I don't want them to lose out. They struggle enough to keep the shop going with everyone using the bigger town over for most of their shopping now."

"We can definitely do that."

"Give me five minutes to get myself sorted and we can go."

Reaper waited by the door and sure enough, five minutes later she was ready, wearing another pair of jeans and flat ankle boots, a pale pink long sleeve top, and a navy Gillet over that.

She dressed like a local, and anyone seeing her wouldn't think for one second that she was the same woman who'd graced magazine covers dripping in diamonds and thousand-pound dresses. It made him wonder who the real Lucía was or if they both lived inside her in a complex mix of the two worlds melded into one life she'd shaped to fit who she was.

Reaper locked the cottage door and activated the alarm to let Watchdog know they were now out of the property. He made to walk for his car, but she turned in the opposite direction.

"We can walk. It's only a few miles and these roads weren't built for that truck."

Her smirk and the little dig at his car made him raise a brow and want to tease her back, but he resisted. Teasing her would be easy. So far being with her this morning had been easy and enjoyable and he needed to pull back from that and remember this was a job, nothing more. He wasn't there to be her friend or her confidant. Much as he craved the need to know her, he knew it would be too dangerous for them both and to keep her safe, he'd need to keep a few walls up.

As he walked silently beside her into the village, his eyes constantly searching for a threat, the mild autumn day pleasant and dry, he thought he felt a tinge of regret at his quietness coming from Lucía but put that down to his own feelings. This was going to be a long six months.

CHAPTER 4

Lucía motioned towards Percy who was a five-year-old Jack Russell rescue. "I think he's getting used to you."

The first day meeting him, Percy had taken an instant dislike to Justice and decided his ankle would be a good target for his teeth. Poor Percy had been no match for Justice though and he'd soon learned there was only one alpha in the room, and it wasn't him.

Now after a full week, not only had Justice won Percy over but Mrs Howard was also completely enamoured, and Mr Jonson treated him like he was his new best friend. Everyone loved him and he was charming and played the role of doting fiancé so well it would be easy to fall into the trap of believing it was real if he didn't lock down like a vice the second they were alone.

"We have an understanding, don't we, Percy?"

"Do you have a dog?"

Justice shook his head. "No, this job doesn't really allow for it, but my teammate does, and as they're part of the team I'm around them a lot."

"What kind?"

"Scout is a German shepherd who's almost entirely black with just a slight tan colour on his chest, and then there's Monty. He's an Australian Shepherd. Scout is calm and very obedient, but Monty is a teenager in dog years and can be overprotective. Val is fantastic with them though. Those dogs would die for her and I'm pretty sure she'd die for them. She and her brother are both dog handlers and trainers."

A prickle of jealousy that was unpleasant and unfounded burrowed into her belly at the fondness with which he spoke about the other woman. "You sound close."

"We are. Not just me and Val. The whole team is close. There's nothing I wouldn't do for them, and I know they'd be there for me in a heartbeat if I needed them. That kind of loyalty should never be taken for granted. It's a precious commodity."

As they rounded the edge of the field on the loop they walked with Percy each day and headed back toward Mrs Howard's home, once again Justice went quiet. All week he'd been pleasant and polite, but she'd seen nothing of the man who'd first arrived and done his utmost to rattle her, and at the same time made her feel alive for the first time in years.

Once they'd handed Percy back to his mum and said a long goodbye to Mrs Howard. With the promise to take lots of pictures next week at the ball, they made the short walk home in silence.

Inside he headed for his room as he did most afternoons and she worked at the table. Opening her laptop, she logged in to her emails and saw a pile to deal with. Before she tackled that mountain, she wanted a cup of tea. Brewing the kettle, she went towards the room Justice used and paused a second before knocking once.

The door flew open and Lucía gasped at the sight before her. Justice was standing in just a towel over his lower half, water dripping down his perfectly sculpted chest in rivulets that she wanted to follow with her tongue. Her eyes moved lower, past rippling abs toward a happy trail that made women around the world weep, and the thick, corded V muscle pointing the way to manna from heaven.

As her eyes hit his crotch she gasped louder at the clear evidence of his erection, the towel doing little to hide what was an impressive bulge. Snapping out of her sex induced stupor, her eyes shot to his smirking face.

"Something I can help you with, Princess?"

Embarrassment burned her cheeks, and she fought the urge to cover her face with her hands, instead, straightening her neck and acting as the royal she was. "Not at all. I came to see if you wanted some tea."

"Some tea would be lovely, Lucía. Now if you're finished staring, I have something I need to take care of."

His words made a heaviness settle in her lower belly; the implication was clear that he was going to be taking care of that erection just two doors away from where she sat.

"You should put some clothes on." Her voice was prudish and snappy as she walked away, her head so high it was a wonder she didn't trip over her own feet, but Lucía was classier than that.

"And maybe you should take that stick from up your ass and find a way to ease some of your own tension. Unless you want us to do that together."

Lucía had never been spoken to the way Justice spoke to her and she hated to admit that it turned her on, making her desperate to take him up on his offer. She wouldn't of course, because she had a feeling once that door was open there would be no closing it. "Go to hell."

"Already there, angel."

The slamming door made her fume as she busied herself making tea and a sandwich she knew she wouldn't eat. Her emotions were too all over the place to eat but she needed to do something to keep her from marching back in that room and climbing that perfectly annoying, sexy asshole like a tree.

Taking the tea and the plate holding her sandwich to the table, she took a moment to compose herself, taking in the beauty of the garden the breakfast nook overlooked. This place was her sanctuary, her place to be herself without the stress of the outside world.

Tomorrow they'd fly to Spain where she'd once more be Princess Lucía, second in line to the throne, on display for all to see. She'd don her uniform and do what was expected of her because that was her job.

Shaking away the annoyance and tension the encounter with Justice had caused, she sipped the camomile tea and let it work its calming magic on her. She felt rather than saw his presence as Justice came into the room, thankfully fully dressed and went about making himself some lunch.

Ignoring him, Lucía began to go through her emails from her work account. She answered each of them, confirming schedules and turning down offers while accepting others. Justice was handling the logistics of her trip, her only role was to turn up and take pictures. Using her fake identity, the same one she'd used since the start of her career, gave her freedom that her real one wouldn't.

Opening the latest email, she scanned the contents and found nothing except a link to a video. She hesitated for a moment, she didn't recognise the sender and was worried the link would have a virus that would screw her system. Deciding it was probably safe as it had got through her fire walls, she clicked to open it.

A grainy image came on the screen, and she leaned closer, squinting to make out what it was. As the screen came into focus Lucía pulled away, bile sliding up her throat and horror swimming in her mind.

A young man, of no more than twenty, was tied to a chair in a dirty, squalid building. His face was filthy and a once-white rag was stuffed in his mouth. His clothes were torn and his feet were bare and almost black with dirt. It was an image she'd seen before, not this one, but many like it as she'd photographed the war in the Middle East.

But this wasn't an image, this was a video and as she watched, two men in dark clothing walked on screen, their faces covered by ski masks. Her gasp must have caught Justice's attention as he stood and walked quickly toward her, but her eyes never left the screen.

"What is it?"

Lucía pointed at the screen. "I was sent this."

His warmth behind her gave her a feeling of security as they watched the man face the camera and speak.

"Do not come here or this will be you, Your Highness."

Then the man lifted what looked like a scythe and swung it at the young man's neck. Before the horror could translate, Justice slammed the laptop closed, cutting off the final evil act from her sight.

Turning her chair to face him, Justice looked her in the eye, his face a mask of calm fury. "Who sent that?"

"I don't know. It was sent to my work email." She could hear the horror in her voice at the fear and despair on the boy's face and the knowledge that he'd die clear in his eyes.

"Fuck."

"Was it real?"

Justice crouched in front of her his hands covering her cold ones. "I don't know, angel, but I'm going to find out."

Justice went to move away, and she held on tight to his hand, not wanting to lose the peace and security she'd found around him. No matter their argument, he made her feel safer than anyone ever had, and she needed that more than anything else in that second.

His blue eyes darkened as he looked at her before sighing and pulling her into his arms and carrying her toward the couch. Sitting, he eased her onto his lap and held her head to his chest as she began to shake. Lucía closed her eyes, trying to get the images from her mind, and like the other horrors she'd witnessed, she knew this one would haunt her too.

Lucía shivered, her entire body succumbing to shock as the reality of what she'd witnessed hit her and Justice held on tighter as if he was holding her together by sheer will. Instead of feeling suffocated, she burrowed closer, sinking into his heat as firm lips pressed to her head.

"We'll figure this out, Lucía, and find out who sent that video and if it's real."

"He was sending me a message. That was for me the Princess, not me the photographer. He called me Your Highness. Very few people know that work is mine."

"I know and from now on I'll be stuck to you like glue. No more walking everywhere. We're taking this seriously."

Lucía pulled away and she could see the sincerity and determination in his eyes when he looked at her and she shivered for a different reason as desire, hot and sharp, lanced through her body. Her nipples beaded as she realised the position they were in and felt the hard ridge of his cock beneath her thighs.

For a moment neither of them moved and she held her breath, not knowing whether she wanted to run away or throw herself at him and demand he give her what she wanted. What she'd needed since the moment he'd walked into her life a week ago and woken every hormone in her body.

Before she could decide, Justice lifted her and set her on the couch before taking a step back. "I need to call my team. Will you be okay?"

"Of course."

Justice nodded and rushed to his room as if he didn't trust her not to attack him and wrestle him to the ground. At least with the carnal images in her head, there was no room for the horror on her laptop.

CHAPTER 5

Reaper slammed the door and banged his head against it in frustration. He'd been so close to saying fuck it and giving into the primal urges he was feeling that were reflected in Lucía's eyes, but he couldn't. After what had just happened, he realised she needed him to keep her safe more than ever, and that had overruled every other instinct.

He hadn't said it, but there was no doubt in his mind the video was real, and it had shown a young man losing his life as a warning to her to stay away. He wanted to march back out there and snatch her up and run, take her someplace safe but it wasn't an option. He knew once the shock wore off for her, she'd only be more determined not to be cowed. The woman he'd come to know this last week had a spine of steal and a heart that was warm and kind but determined to do right by people. It was a humbling thing to know he'd been so wrong about her. He fought the instinct to like her because he knew it could be a slippery slope from liking her to wanting her with every breath in his body.

Dialling the number, he got straight through to Bás. "We have a fucking problem."

Bás growled. "If you fucked her, I'm gonna bury you on this fucking mountain."

"Calm down. I haven't laid a finger on her." Not strictly true but close enough not to have him going to hell for lying. No, he was going to hell for many other reasons.

"Then what?"

"She just got an email sent to her professional account with the video of a young man being beheaded."

"Jesus Christ."

"Yeah, exactly and it gets worse. There were two men on the video, covered head to toe in black fatigues. The one who seemed to be the leader addressed her as Your Highness when he warned her to stay away or she'd be next."

"Where's the laptop now?"

"In the living room."

Reaper could hear Bás walking and knew exactly where he was going.

"Get it so Watchdog can take it over and see what he can find."

Reaper walked back into the main living room to find Lucía nowhere in sight. He figured she'd either retreated to her room or was in the bathroom. Sitting at the table he woke the sleeping laptop. "I'm putting you on speaker."

"Reaper, I need you to give me remote access to this laptop. You need to go to this website."

Reaper typed in the web address Watchdog gave him and a command popped up on the screen. He followed each of the directions knowing if there was something to find, Watchdog would find it. As the video played again in front of him, he watched it to the end, knowing the team were doing the same on the other end.

"Shit, that's cold."

Lotus was hardly warm and fuzzy, but he could hear the disgust in her voice at the violent act of ending the man's life.

"Is it real?" he asked, already knowing deep down what the answer would be.

"Without a doubt."

"Can you find anything from the metadata or the men in it?"

"If it's there I'll find it."

"Thanks." Reaper knew that was the truth. If Watchdog couldn't find it, then it wasn't there to be found.

"This changes everything going forward. I'll need to contact the King and tell him about this."

"No, wait. Let me speak to him tomorrow in person. By then I'll have more information and a better idea of the threat and I can give him a detailed plan. If we tell him now, he'll pull the plug and stop Lucía from going on her trip."

"And rightly so. She's in real danger."

Reaper knew Bás was right, but he also knew how stubborn Lucía was and how upset she'd be not to go, and he wanted to find a way for her to get what she wanted. "I know, but if he pulls the plug, it still doesn't guarantee her safety. Very few people know who she is in the outside world, which means it's someone close to her."

"You have twenty-four hours to tell him or I'll call him myself."

"That's all I need. Just find out everything you can, Watchdog."

"On it like a car bonnet."

Reaper smiled knowing Watchdog was already working, his brain was so much quicker than anyone else he knew.

Bás came back on the line. "You're off speaker. Do you need backup?"

"No, this village is as safe as houses. They adore her so nobody gets past them. Plus all the residents passed every single background check we ran and so did their family members. We fly to the Palace tomorrow, and she'll have the Palace Guard as added security."

"We don't know if we can trust them."

"I know. Which is why I'll be stuck to her like glue. Our cover helps but not inside the Palace where the fake identities don't work."

"How will you ensure she stays safe?"

"Come on, Bás. You know better than to ask that but rest assured where she goes, I go. Inside and outside the Palace grounds."

"If the King catches you in her room, he'll cut your balls off."

"Maybe, maybe not. If he understands the threat could be internal, he might approve it."

"Or I could send Duchess over to help or perhaps Valentina? She'd blend in with the other guests and would be an easier sell for the King."

Reaper wanted to refuse. He wanted to be the one protecting Lucía, but he knew that was stupid and this was a better option. "Good idea. Valentina would be perfect. Get the King to approve it and I'll give him the details tomorrow when we arrive."

"Talk soon."

Bás hung up and Reaper left the laptop running as the mouse moved around the screen while Watchdog did his thing. Movement from the corner of the room caught his eye and he glanced up to see Lucía watching him from the hallway that led to the bedrooms.

"Thank you."

Reaper stood and walked closer being careful to keep some space between them so he didn't give into the urge to pull her into his arms. "What for?"

"For fighting in my corner."

Reaper shrugged. "I just don't want people making gut-punch reactions."

"Well, I appreciate it anyway."

"You're welcome."

He moved away into the kitchen, flicking the TV on as he passed the remote, not wanting the silence in the room opening like a gorge between them. An old episode of *Friends* came on and filled the silence with canned laughter.

"What would you like for dinner?"

For the last week, they'd eaten separately. He'd felt it was safer to keep the barrier between them, but he knew that wasn't what she needed tonight, and if he was honest, he didn't want to be alone either.

"You don't have to cook. I can grab some cheese and crackers or fruit."

Reaper gave her a warning look. "Cheese and crackers are a snack, not dinner. How about I make my mum's famous beef burgers?"

She moved closer and he could tell she was relaxing. "Why are they famous?"

"Because she told me they were, and I don't argue with my mother."

Lucía laughed and he grinned back at her infectious smile.

"Okay sounds good but let me help. I might want to steal the recipe if it's that good."

"Fine, grab the minced beef from the fridge and I'll show you but don't tell anyone. It's a closely guarded secret and I'm only telling you because you're my fake wife."

"Fair point."

They worked side by side, the conversation on innocent topics such as movies, TV shows, favourite food, likes, and dislikes. It was easy and Reaper found himself enjoying spending time with an attractive woman he wanted in his bed without it being his only thought.

He liked Lucía the person, not the Princess but the woman who walked dogs for old ladies and made sure to spend money in the local shop to keep an older couple from going under.

For the rest of the evening, they ate delicious burgers that had turned out even better than usual, and that was saying a lot as it was his signature dish. They watched *Friends* on TV until around nine when Lucía began to yawn, covering her face with the back of her hand.

"You should get to bed."

"I know. It's been a long day, but I'm not sure I'll sleep once my head hits the pillow. It's usually the time my brain wakes up and decides it's the time to fix every problem under the sun."

"You always been this way?"

Lucía shook her head. "No. As a child, I'd put my head down and be out within minutes. It drove Maria crazy because she was never like that."

"When did it change?"

Lucía shrugged. "Not sure. I just grew up I guess."

"Yeah, I get that."

"What about you?"

"I learned to sleep on the side of a mountain in the military, but never for very long. Even now I only sleep for about four or five hours."

"What a pair we are."

"Yeah, crazy insomniacs."

Lucía went quiet and he wondered what she was thinking and hoped her mind hadn't gone to the video from earlier but knew she had.

"Was it real, Justice?"

He could lie to her but knew he wouldn't. "Yes."

She nodded, her arms were crossed over her midriff as if holding everything inside her. "I knew it was. I just hoped."

"We'll find them, Lucía, you have my word."

"I know, but that boy will still be dead because of me."

Reaper stood, not wanting to hear her blame herself and crossed to her, taking her shoulders in his hands, and gently turning her so she was looking at him. "This isn't your fault. Those men did this for their own evil reasons. You can't blame yourself for the actions of others. It will eat you up and spit you out."

"But this *was* my fault. It happened because of me."

"No."

"Yes!"

"No, God dammit. Don't do this, please."

"Why not?"

"Because I know what it does to you."

"How?"

Reaper never bared his soul, but this felt like the only way to make her understand. "Because when I was in the military, the men under my command did something horrific and for a long time, I blamed their actions on myself and in some ways I always will. But I don't want that for you."

"I'm sorry that happened but it's not the same. They didn't do it because of you."

"Neither did these men. You're the excuse, the pawn. They did this for their own sick agenda."

"I want to believe you."

"Then believe me. This isn't your fault any more than it was the kid's fault for being in the wrong place at the wrong time. What ifs will eat you up inside."

"I know. My logical brain knows everything you're saying is true, but my heart is just going to take time to catch up."

"Well then, it's a good thing I'm around to keep you honest."

"I'm not sure you're going to keep me honest, but you certainly helped today, so thank you."

"You're welcome. Now get yourself to bed. We have a long day tomorrow."

Lucía saluted him. "Sir, yes, sir."

He watched her saunter away towards her bedroom. It took everything in him not to follow her and spend the entire night making sure the only thing she thought about was pleasure. But that wasn't his role, and it never would be. She was a Princess, and he was just her lowly bodyguard.

CHAPTER 6

As THE PLANE GOT CLOSER AND CLOSER TO HER HOMELAND, SHE COULD FEEL the tension growing in her shoulders. Looking out at the beautiful deep azure of the Mediterranean Sea, she was filled with a sense of love for the land and the people she served. Lucía loved her country, was passionate about it and the people, but it was the politics and rules which chaffed against her skin.

The second the plane landed she was bombarded by people wanting things from her. Justice led her from the private plane toward the waiting car, his hand resting on her back, his body alert to any danger, his head on a constant swivel looking for an attack. He didn't allow a chance for her fear to overtake her. She knew without a single doubt that he'd protect her with his life, and that hadn't always been the case with the men guarding her.

All of them wanted to be on Maria's duty. The second in line was a mere inconvenience to so many. As Justice opened the car door she smothered a groan at the sight of the King's private secretary, Felix Morales, sitting in the back waiting for her.

Justice tensed and pushed his body in front of her. "Who the fuck are you?"

Felix bristled, his perfectly plucked eyebrows almost jumping off his face in surprised indignance, the pout of annoyance as he looked down his nose at Justice made her angry on his behalf. "I'm the King's private secretary, and you'll address me with respect."

Justice held the door open and hooked his thumb behind him, making it clear what he was saying. "Out."

"I beg your pardon?"

"You heard me. Out of the car now before I toss you out myself."

Lucía rolled her lips to keep from laughing out loud. She detested Felix and had no idea why her father kept him around. The man was a manipulative climber who used his position to further his own pocket.

"You have no right," Felix spluttered glaring at her with open hostility as if she'd said the words which so affronted him.

"I have every right. I'm her bodyguard and I wasn't made aware you'd be riding with us. Therefore, you won't be."

"Lucía?"

Felix looked to her for support, but he'd find none there. He'd never done anything but give her barely veiled, snide comments all the while fluttering around her sister like she was the most perfect being on earth. Lucía got it, her sister was heir apparent and was therefore treated with deference. She even did it herself sometimes.

If her sister had been a different person, the behaviour would've made her into a not very nice human being, but she was truly wonderful and genuinely kind. They were close in age with just eighteen months between them and their affection for each other was open and loving.

"It's Princess Lucía or Your Highness." Lucía had reminded Felix of this more than once, but the man only seemed to remember when he was around other, higher-ranked, members of the family.

At fifty-eight, Felix Morales was a handsome man who was tall with grey hair and a neatly trimmed grey beard. She knew he was popular with the ladies but also why he'd never married. His whole life was a lie, and she'd feel sorry for him keeping his sexuality a secret if he hadn't been such an utter bastard to her.

As his face contorted in rage, Justice leaned in as if he was truly going to toss him on his ass.

"Do not touch me." Felix exited the car, hatred brimming in every pore as he glared at Justice. "You've made an enemy of me this day."

"Well, shit, now I'm terrified." Justice turned his back on the man and ushered her in the vehicle before closing the door on him.

As the car pulled away, the tension released by the short exchange and a man she disliked getting his comeuppance dissipated. "You shouldn't have done that. Felix can be quite spiteful and will make your life difficult now."

Justice glanced across the car at her as they made their way from the airport to the Palace. He was dressed more formally today in a dark navy suit and white shirt with a grey tie. She was also dressed for her role in a Chanel skirt suit in palest blush, with a cream blouse and nude Gianvito Rossi pumps.

"I honestly couldn't care less about that petty little man and his threats. I've pissed off harder men than him. What I'm interested in is the way he spoke to you."

Lucía sighed, feeling a headache pulling at the base of her neck and moving upwards. Travelling, or maybe it was coming home, always made her feel this way. "Felix is a typical social climber. He believes his position gives him some sort of power and has always treated me that way."

"And your father allows it?"

Justice sounded ready to commit murder and she knew she needed to calm him down before they arrived and he got himself fired or thrown in jail for assaulting the King of Spain.

"No, of course not. He has no idea. Felix never acts out in front of him, and I never give him the satisfaction of running to my father. But let's just say when my sister becomes Queen, his days are numbered."

Justice didn't reply just huffed and she hoped the issue was

45

handled. She didn't have the mental capacity to deal with this right now.

Rolling through the gates of the Palace she was struck again by the beauty of the architecture and the gardens. Opulence and nature lived side by side in harmony in a way that wasn't easy to replicate.

Stopping outside the main entrance, Lucía took a deep breath as Justice exited first to open her door. Protocol had been ingrained into her for so long that slipping back into the role was an easy transition, or at least she hoped she made it seem that way.

The door opened and she got out of the car, a wide smile for the household staff who'd converged to meet her. She greeted each one by name and asked after their families, taking the time to reacquaint herself with each of them. Like the village she liked to call home now, it was the Palace staff who were her true allies amongst the Felix's of this world.

The housekeeper, who'd been with them since she was ten years old, greeted her with a curtsey. "Your Highness, it's good to have you home."

"Thank you. It's good to be home." Justice stayed behind her as she walked through the Palace, the footman bringing her luggage behind her. "Is my sister in residence?"

Maria, her husband, and her young son lived on a property on the Palace grounds. Lucas Cortez was a lawyer and a Duke, and the match with her sister couldn't be more perfect. Especially because it was a love match and that filled Lucía with joy. Her parents' marriage hadn't been. Theirs had been an arranged marriage, but love had grown for them both. Her sister had chosen her husband and the man who would stand beside her when she took on the most difficult role of her life.

"She is and will be at dinner tonight."

"Is it formal?"

"Yes, Princess Lucía."

As she reached her room and her endurance, she turned to thank her staff, including Justice. She'd leave him at her door as she'd done with her previous guards, as the royal security was now in charge of her safety.

But he pushed past her, making the housekeeper gasp. Lucía smiled and dismissed her with a smile, watching as the woman rushed off casting worried glances over her shoulder.

Marching into her suite, she shut the door with more care than she was feeling and faced Justice as he walked through her rooms checking every nook and cranny. "What are you doing?"

He looked at her like she was the one with two heads. "My job."

"You don't need to. The household security will take care of things from here on in, so you can relax."

Justice stalked toward her, and she stepped back, the powerful predator in him barely concealed by the sharp, expensive suit. He stopped barely a breath away from her and she felt her pulse hammering in her neck like a beacon to the nerves and desire she was feeling at his proximity. "Like hell I will. You're my job twenty-four-seven until I'm fired or dead. That means inside the Palace and out."

"That's ridiculous. I'm safe here."

Justice gaped and she would've laughed had he not looked so angry. "Are you that blind, Princess?"

Lucía's hands flew to her hips as her own temper flared now. "What the hell does that mean?"

"It means, Princess, that only a very few people know your other identity and they all live here. Felix has already made it more than clear he holds nothing but disdain for you and your title. It wouldn't be that much of stretch to think he'd sell you out for a decent paycheque."

"I hadn't considered that the leak was inside the Palace." Her fingernail went to her mouth as she began to pace, the ramifications of such a betrayal were huge and it meant she couldn't trust anyone.

Justice stopped her, his hand on her arm as he gently tugged the pinkie on her left hand from her mouth. "No need for self-mutilation, Princess, just breathe."

He led her toward the couch that faced the gardens and she sat heavily, her aching feet sighing in relief. Justice sat beside her, not touching her but close enough she could smell the cologne he wore, which was fresh and manly just like the man himself.

"I didn't tell you to scare you. I told you so you'd be cautious and understand why I'll be on duty even here. I plan to speak with your father about what happened yesterday and give him all the information we have so far."

"Which is?"

"Not a lot, but we've identified the man who was killed as Morgan Litchfield. He was a twenty-two-year-old grad student studying at Durham University. He was also selling drugs and had two assault charges that had been buried by his family, so hardly a stand-up guy."

"Even so, he didn't deserve to die."

"Agreed, but we're closer. We can chase down the men on the video through him and find out who they are and arrest them."

Lucía nodded wringing her hands in her lap. "My father still won't be happy about you being in here. He hand-picked the head of security himself and this will be personal. Plus, the fact you're here will give the wrong impression to everyone about us."

Justice's jaw hardened a tick making him seem angry and she wanted to take her words back.

"I didn't mean...."

He held his hand up. "I know what you meant and you're right, which is why Bás is sending Valentina over to stand in for me when I can't be close enough. She'll check your rooms here and be a second set of eyes for me at the ball."

"Valentina?"

"Yes, she's lovely. You'll like her."

Lucía felt the ugly kernel of jealousy pop inside her chest at his words regarding the woman she'd never met. "I'm sure she's perfect."

Justice looked at her with an unasked question in his eyes, but she refused to embarrass herself further by explaining her catty comment.

"Well, your room is clear and I have an appointment to speak with your father in ten minutes. Do you need to leave your room again before dinner?"

Lucía shook her head. "No, thank you. I think I'll take a bath and get this travel grime off me."

"Then I'll be back at six forty-five to introduce you to Val and escort you to dinner."

Lucía walked him to the door and he turned, his face so close she could see the light silver swirls that moved through the blue of his irises. It would take nothing for her to lean in and kiss him, to take what she wanted instead of holding back but she knew it was pointless to taste something she could never have.

"Lock the door and don't let anyone but me inside until I figure out who we can trust."

"I hate this."

Justice gripped her chin, and she closed her eyes as his thumb rubbed over her bottom lip. "I know, angel, and it will be over soon. For now, just hang tight and do as I ask, okay?"

"Okay."

He paused for a second and she thought he was going to kiss her, but he stepped away taking his warmth with him. "Good girl."

Lucía locked the door and leaned against it before she kicked off her heels and went to run a bath. At least she could still enjoy that.

CHAPTER 7

REAPER HAD NEVER BEEN SO ANGRY IN HIS LIFE AND AT THAT POINT, HE wasn't even sure who he was pissed at. Walking swiftly through the stunning rooms of the Palace, he noted down security breach after security breach.

The second Lucía walked out of her bedroom at the cottage that morning, he'd seen the difference in her. Oh, the clothes were different, but it wasn't that. She looked beautiful no matter what she wore, and he had a feeling her naked would be his absolute favourite, but it was more her demeanour.

The easy-going woman who'd chatted with the villagers and helped the elderly with their shopping was gone, replaced by a stressed, tense, uptight person with a cool detachment. The closer they got to her home of birth, the worse that had become. He could hardly fathom it until that prick Felix had spoken to her as he had and treated her with such open disrespect.

The man was lucky he still had a head on his shoulders because he'd wanted to rip the fucker off. He'd expected some backstabbing and snideness inside a place like this. It was riddled with people who thought their shit didn't stink, but such outright hostility wasn't to be tolerated, at least by him.

Crossing the courtyard, he made his way past suited staff who cast him wary looks as they went about their duties. There was an undercurrent he couldn't quite put his finger on, but he'd find out what it was.

He knocked on the door of the security manager's office and waited, his foot tapping in agitation. The security chief should have been at the airport to meet and brief him, that was the first issue. The second was that the guard didn't patrol the inside of the house or allow personal protection officers to guard their principal inside the Palace.

No answer there, so Reaper gave up and turned to head to the meeting with the King. Might as well take this up with the organ grinder, and if Felix was there so much the better, because he had a few things to say to him, too. He suspected people tiptoed around the man, perhaps in fear or maybe something else. Either way, Felix was about to find out he didn't scare so easy and certainly not from a weak prick like him who bullied people.

His phone rang and he answered as he walked. "Yep."

"It's me."

"I know, Bás. I saw the name on the screen."

"We're at the gate and someone called Felix won't let us inside."

"Motherfucker. Okay, let me handle this and call you back. Just hang tight."

Reaper increased his speed, wondering why Bás was there but knowing Bás would tell him if he wanted him to know.

The King was in his drawing room and Reaper waited outside while a guard on the door announced him. That, at least, was something in their favour. The King was properly guarded, or was that insulated? The two might seem the same but had very different roles and outcomes in his mind.

"The King will see you now," a uniformed and armed guard no less, told him.

Reaper nodded and stepped inside, dropping his head in a bow as the King greeted him. Tall and lean with dark hair like his daughter's, just speckled with grey, he had a strong jaw and dark eyes and looked every inch the part. His suit was pristine with the crest of his house over his shoulder.

"Mr Carson, it's good to finally meet you in person."

"The honour is mine, Your Majesty."

The King held his hand out to a brocade chair in ruby red. "Please, sit."

Reaper waited for the King to sit first before taking a chair opposite him. Felix was standing behind the King, his glare aimed at Reaper, but his mouth firmly closed. The man would never run his mouth in front of the King. No, he was more devious than that.

"Might I speak with you alone?"

The King angled his head before nodding and turning to Felix to dismiss him.

"Your Majesty, I really must object after what we discussed."

"Leave us." The King's voice was deep and calm but showed who was in charge and left no room for argument, not that anyone would.

Felix cast him an open glare before he nodded, dipping his head in a bow, and leaving via a different door from the one Reaper had entered.

"I trust you and my daughter are getting along better now?"

"We are, sir, and I apologised to her and now you if my behaviour was out of line. It was never my intention to upset the Princess."

"I'm sure. Now, I assume you're not here to discuss incidentals. So, tell me what is on your mind."

Reaper liked the directness and respected a man who could cut to the chase. "Yesterday the Princess received an email to her work account containing a video of a man being beheaded. The killers, three men who we're trying to identify, threatened her to stay away and addressed her by her royal title."

The King stood and walked so he was behind the chair, leaning on it slightly as he did. "Is she okay?"

"She was shaken but she's a strong woman and if I may say so, stubborn. She won't allow us to stop her plans and I fear doing so won't help in any case."

"Why not? Surely if she were to come home she'd be safe."

Reaper knew this could go down very badly but he had to be honest, he knew no other way. "Permission to speak freely?"

"Of course, I have enough sycophants. I don't need one protecting Lucía too."

Reaper smothered a smile at the King's response. "The men knew her title, which means they knew who she was. As far as I'm aware there are only a handful of people who know that Lucía is Carla Cassidy, war photographer. Which means the leak came from inside the Palace. Apart from that, the security here isn't up to par, I hate to say it, but I don't believe she's safe here, so much so that Bás and another female operative have flown over. Although Felix won't let them through the gate."

"You believe she's in danger here?"

"I do."

"I'll have Felix escort Bás and the other person inside personally and apologise to them, but I fear he was just being overprotective. He can be a bit much sometimes."

Reaper could hardly contain his anger as he remembered the way he'd spoken to her at the airport. "He's more than that. He's rude and disrespectful to your daughter."

The King's jaw clenched, and he could tell he wasn't happy, but Reaper didn't care, he needed to know. "He addresses her by her given name, talks down to her, and won't allow her personal guard inside the house, decreeing that the household guard handle it. That's not good enough for her. She may only be the 'spare to the heir' as he calls her, but she's a human being who deserves respect from him."

"Why has Lucía never mentioned this to me?"

"You'd need to speak with her and ask her yourself, but her sister is aware of the situation."

"I'll speak to my head of security about this and make sure you're allowed inside with her at all times, but I must insist that you not enter her bed chambers."

Reaper didn't rate his head of security for shit but held his tongue. He'd got away with everything so far and pushing his luck with a man such as this would never work. "Of course. Which is why I've asked for a female operative. Valentina will stay by the Princess's side when I can't."

"What about the rest of the household? Do you believe the threat is just against Lucía?"

"I do. I think it stems back to her work and perhaps something she's seen, or they're afraid of what she may uncover. She's an excellent and talented woman and may know something these people don't want exposed. That said, I think it's prudent for everyone to increase their security for the time being until these people are caught and the leak found and plugged."

"Do we know anything about these people?"

"We believe they're white males, with military training, most likely special ops, and have seen combat. Other than that we have very little, but we're searching through every thread we can to expose them."

"And Lucía? She's aware of all of this?"

"She is. As I said, she's a strong, intelligent woman and I think honesty is the best way for her to handle things."

"You seem to have got the measure of my daughter in a very short period of time, Mr Carson."

Was that suspicion in the King's tone or was it his own guilt at the feeling of lust and desire he felt for the Princess? "It's my job to read people. She's easy to read as she wears her heart on her sleeve."

"Really? Most say she's a closed book, but you seem to have seen a different person than she shows to others outside her family."

"On the contrary, she's warm and friendly to those in her village and is loved by them all."

"She's safe there? I worry about her being all alone and far away but as you've most likely seen, she's stubborn and independent."

"She's very safe there. The people love her and as it's so close-knit, nobody gets past the neighbourhood watch. She has her own personal army with the villagers."

The King seemed pleased by this news. "Good. Will you join Lucía as her escort to dinner and to the ball tomorrow? I'd feel happier knowing she has someone with her at all times."

"Of course, it would be my pleasure and as I said, Bás and Valentina will also be there in the background."

"Thank you, Mr Carson. Please keep me abreast of the situation and I will handle the other things we talked about on my end."

Reaper nodded and stood, making his exit, pleased the King had listened and taken on board what he'd said. He didn't know if he believed him about Felix but the King had the knowledge now and could speak to Princess Maria to corroborate if he so wished. He only cared about Lucía and how she was treated, and in front of him it would be with respect or heads would fucking roll.

Wanting to take a shower, but knowing he needed to brief Bás and Valentina on his meeting with the King first, he headed for the gate.

CHAPTER 8

Stepping into the black satin heel of her Jimmy Choo's, Lucía felt marginally better after the relaxing soak in the bath. The scented bubbles and hot water soothed her tense body. The last thirty-six hours had been testing, to say the least, but time alone brought perspective. She knew that she could either allow this to get to her and let these assholes win or fight back, and she was nothing if not a fighter.

A knock on her door had her tummy fluttering with nerves as she smoothed the non-existent wrinkles from her calf-length, A-line skirt made from black silk. A fitted blouse of deep teal that she'd paired with it complimented her complexion. Answering the door, she pasted on a smile as Justice looked at her from head to toe, his gaze moving slowly in appreciation before landing on her face.

"You look beautiful, Princess Lucía."

Lucía inclined her head. "Why thank you, kind sir, you look very handsome yourself." And he did in a dark grey suit and white shirt, with a deep green tie that almost matched her top. She knew she shouldn't compliment him nor he, her. It was against protocol for them to be so familiar, but she didn't care about that at this moment.

Justice made her feel giddy like this was a date when really, it was dinner with her family.

"Shall we?"

He held out his hand for her to proceed him and she nodded, wishing she could take his hand or his arm instead, but he wasn't hers to have and never would be. That thought made her sad, not because she'd fallen in love with him or anything crazy. They'd barely known each other a week and most of that was spent fighting or being civil, the other half giving each other searing looks which would scorch the earth. It might be worth it to take his arm if it gave Felix a coronary because the little man certainly wouldn't approve of that.

"What are you smiling at?"

Lucía bit her lip and grinned wider. "Nothing."

"Secrets will get you in trouble, Princess Lucía."

She stopped at the top of the stairs and turned to him. "Justice, promise me when we're alone it's just Lucía."

She didn't want to be a Princess around him, she just wanted to be herself.

As if understanding, he nodded. "Of course."

"Did you meet with my father?"

"I did and he knows everything."

Lucía sighed in resignation. "Did he pull the plug on my trip?"

"Not at all. He fully understands what it means to you and wants it to go ahead as long as it's safe."

That surprised her and she wondered how much of that was Justice's doing, but she didn't betray any of her thoughts openly. "And will it be? Safe that is."

Justice stopped outside the dining room door and touched her arm, before pulling away. "Lucía, I promise you on my life I won't let anything happen to you."

"Okay."

"Okay? Just like that?"

"I trust you so if you say it's okay it will be. If you say it isn't then I'll worry, but you need to promise you'll be honest with me."

"I'll always be honest with you."

"Good, that's important to me. There are too many lies and untruths in the world, or at least in mine, and I hate it."

"I know you do."

Justice opened the door and instead of leaving her, he followed her inside. Before she could say anything, she was swept up in hugs from her family. Her sister, looking sensational in a burgundy shift dress with lace at the wrists, rushed toward her.

Her sister's embrace was like coming home and she hugged her tight before pulling back and assessing Lucía as she'd always done, the eighteen-month age gap meaning Maria took on the older sister mantle and ran with it. "Lucía, oh I've missed you."

"I've missed you too. How is my gorgeous nephew?"

"A little rascal like his father." Maria beamed at the man who walked up behind her and leaned in to kiss her cheek.

"Lucía, good to see you."

"You too, Lucas. How is work?"

Lucía liked Lucas and adored how much he loved her sister. He was a kind intelligent man and they often talked shop when they were together. He'd been a human rights lawyer and she often asked him for advice on matters for the charity.

"Busy as always but you know I wouldn't have it any other way."

As they chatted, she saw Justice talking to a man and a woman she didn't recognise. The man was tall with reddish-blond hair and a powerful build. The way he kept glancing around the room told her he was probably one of Justice's colleagues.

The woman was stunning with long dark hair, high cheek bones, ruby red lips, and a smile that was both genuine and seductive. Slim with long legs, she wore a navy shift dress, gold heeled pumps, and a three-quarter length sleeve cropped jacket over the top of the dress, giving her a professional and yet sexy look.

As Justice laughed at something she said Lucía felt the punch of jealousy in her belly, a proprietary feeling of ownership about a man she'd never even kissed and knew she was a fool.

"He's very handsome."

Lucía started and turned to her sister who was grinning at her and watching Justice. Waving her hand in a whatever motion she laughed. "He is but he's my bodyguard, so off-limits. I'm not actually sure why he's here."

"Didn't you hear? Daddy sent a missive earlier today that all personal protection officers would now be engaged to stay with their principal, and no part of the Palace is off-limits for them apart from the bedrooms, and then a female PPO must check the rooms."

"Oh, wow. I had no idea."

"Yes, he also asked me about Felix's treatment of you over the years and I told him the truth."

Lucía gasped, taking her sister's hand. "You did?"

"Yes, of course. He behaves abominably towards you. Father was furious and I'll be surprised if Felix isn't hiding somewhere with his tail between his legs."

Lucía looked to Justice to find him watching her, and a feeling of overwhelming gratitude and something more she couldn't identify spread through her chest. When he looked at her as he did now, he made her feel like she was the only woman in the world.

"I think your hunky bodyguard had something to do with it."

"Yes, perhaps you're right."

Before her sister could say more, the doors opened and her mother and father entered, as the rest of the room dropped into respectful bows or curtseys.

Her mother looked radiant in a cream lace dress with pink flowers overlaid, and her father wore a navy suit with his family insignia embroidered on the left lapel. They approached her and she let her father pull her into a tight hug which somehow always seemed to fix the wrongs of the world. His lips against her hair were familiar, his cologne the one he'd worn her entire life, making her think of happier times.

"Mi hija, it's so good to see you."

He pulled away, and as Maria had done, he looked her over, assessing she was well. "You look well."

"I am well."

"We'll speak about things after dinner but for now it's good you're home, and I'm happy you're safe." He glanced behind her with a nod, and she followed his gaze, seeing him looking at Justice and the other two.

"Your security team will be joining us for dinner, and I've asked Mr Carson to escort you to the ball tomorrow night."

"Really?"

"I'd feel happier knowing he's beside you."

Lucía wanted to bounce on her toes with excitement at the thought but tamped it down, knowing he was just doing his job and it wasn't some fairy tale.

Her father turned his attention to Maria and Lucas, and she greeted her mother who enthused about her outfit and talked about her latest charity event. Soon she was called away to speak to her aunt who'd arrived with her uncle and cousin.

Not wanting to get pulled into the melee, she stepped back, taking a glass of champagne from the waiter.

"Princess Lucía, I'd like for you to meet my friends Bás and Valentina."

Lucía shook their hands and smiled. "It's nice to meet you both."

"The pleasure is ours, Princess Lucía. If you need anything please don't hesitate to ask. Val will be beside you whenever Reaper can't."

"It's lovely to meet you."

As Valentina beamed at her, Lucía had a feeling it would be difficult to dislike this woman. "Justice tells me you train dogs."

She saw Bás and Val exchange a look before Val nodded. "I do. I currently have Scout and Monty."

"A German Shepherd and an Australian Shepherd, right?"

Val beamed wider. "Yes, that's correct. Scout is my calm one,

Monty is more of a handful, but we're getting there now he's passed the wild teenage stage."

As the woman talked, Lucía found herself really liking her and enjoying her company. She might only be there because she was paid but she was friendly and put her at ease which was welcomed.

"I've seen your photographs, and I must say they're devastating in their beauty and poignancy and so thought-provoking. I remember seeing one of a little boy amongst the rubble of the earthquake in Haiti holding his toy car and it made me cry. The destruction we cause to the earth as humans is surely coming back to bite us, and I think seeing these pictures does more to alter a person's mindset than all the nagging about recycling."

"Oh, a woman after my own heart. You must sit with me at dinner so we can chat more." Lucía took Val's arm and led her to the dining room table as the bell rang to say the meal was ready.

For the first time that day, she was starving. The nerves and dread that had plagued her were gone as she was surrounded by people who would insulate her from vague, catty comments about her life and lack of a husband.

Once seated she found Justice on one side and Val on the other, with Bás on the other side of Val. Her father had the head of the table and her mother the seat to his left, with Maria taking the seat to his right as heir.

There was always a hierarchy and she was happy with her position. It was others who made it hard for her to forget or not care. They seemed to care more than she did.

Dinner was lovely, the dishes she'd loved as a child were served with her favourite wine. Justice kept his attention on her most of the meal, only answering questions as they were addressed to him. He wasn't flirtatious in any way and was a perfect gentleman. She found although she liked this Justice, she preferred the real him who'd taught her how to cook burgers and laughed at the same *Friends'* jokes while he sat with his feet on the coffee table.

"Lucía, have you found a match yet or are you still flitting about like you have no responsibilities to this family?"

A hush rang around the room at her aunt's words, and she saw her cousin Amelia, who was only two years younger and engaged to be married, smirk. Lucía felt her ears burn with embarrassment, hating that the attention was once again on her and her failings, and this time Justice was there to see it. That shouldn't matter to her, but it did, and she felt tears well in her eyes.

He tensed beside her, and she shook her head, knowing he was about to defend her and that it would only bring more questions than answers.

CHAPTER 9

Fury thrummed through him as the woman he knew to be the King's younger sister made her barbed comment. Glancing around the room, which was now so quiet he could hear a pin drop, he waited for someone to say something. When it appeared the vile woman's words would go unchallenged, he went to speak, only for Lucía to lay her hand on his arm and give him a look of warning.

Reaper wasn't a fool. He knew making a scene would likely cause more harm than good, but he couldn't fathom why the daggers were out for this amazing and kind woman, and why nobody was standing up for her.

His eyes found the King watching him as if he too was waiting. Reaper clenched his jaw so hard, he was sure his next dentist bill would be in the thousands as he tried not to say anything but lost the battle. Throwing his napkin on the table he stood. "My apologies but I can't sit here and listen to Princess Lucía take these nastily veiled questions any longer. Since we arrived, I've seen her spoken to with rudeness, disdain, dismissal, and open hostility. I have no idea why I, a virtual stranger, am the only one willing to stand up for her."

"Justice, please."

He glanced down at the heated cheeks and saw her shame and the way her shoulders huddled over as if she was trying to disappear. "I'm sorry, Princess Lucía, but it's the truth."

The sound of someone clapping made him look up to see it was Princess Maria. "Bravo. It's about time someone said something."

"And who, pray tell, are you to speak to me like that? I'm a Princess, and you're a nobody. At least my niece knows her place." The woman, who would've been attractive if not for the pinched face and multitude of plastic surgeries she'd clearly had, asked him as she looked down her nose.

"I'm..."

"He's my guest and he's correct."

Reaper looked at the King who was eyeing him, not his sister.

"We've allowed Lucía to be treated as less. Not by lack of love on my part or her mother's, but nonetheless, it has happened. For that, I'm sorry, Lucía. You're a valued member of this family, as valued as any other and if it has not seemed thus then I'm truly sorry."

He looked at his sister then. "As for her duty, Lucía does her duty better than anyone I know and I doubt her mother or sister would disagree. It's just, unlike some people, she doesn't flaunt her efforts for all to see."

Violetta rose. "How dare you speak to me in such a manner."

Her meek husband stood as well after his wife's comment, and their daughter, who'd been smirking at her mother's comments towards Lucía, now looked horrified.

"I dare because I am your King and this is my home. If you can't be civil to my family then leave. I won't tolerate any more of this nonsense in my house, and that goes for anyone who thinks they can speak to my child in such a way."

"Daddy, it's okay."

He realised then Lucía was a peacemaker. That was why she'd allowed herself to be treated in such a way and it was probably why she photographed the wars and horrors as she did, in an effort to do her bit for peace.

"No, mi hija, it's not. I should have dealt with this before. Mr Carson is right, and I thank him for bringing this to my attention. I'm just sorry he had to do so."

Lucía nodded, her head down as her aunt and her family swept from the room.

"You know where to find me when you wish to apologise, my King." The sarcasm in Violetta's voice was evident as she left.

The King ignored her outburst and resumed his meal as if the last few minutes hadn't happened.

Reaper sat and turned to Lucía. "Are you okay?"

"Yes."

She wasn't and he could see it, but he let her have her silence knowing that when she was ready to speak, she would.

Valentina quickly engaged her in a conversation about her charities and before long it was as if the harsh words exchanged hadn't happened.

"Mr Carson, tell me, did you always want to be a bodyguard or was it something you fell into?" Princess Maria addressed him with a warm smile so similar to her sister's, it was easy to see the resemblance.

"Not always, Your Highness, it's more a case of the job chose me."

They chatted for a bit longer as dessert was brought out and she asked about his travels and if he missed his home. All the while he could feel the burn of Bás' eyes in the back of his head. He'd catch hell for his behaviour and he'd need to make things right with the King before the night was over. Because despite the King backing him he knew he'd overstepped, and he could pull him off this job. He didn't trust anyone to guard Lucía better than himself, not even his teammates. And wasn't that telling to how he was feeling about her, despite his constant denial that she was just a job, a beautiful one, but just a job.

As everyone stood to retire to the drawing room, Bás caught his arm and held him back as Valentina walked beside Lucía. "What the fuck was that?"

"I know. I'm sorry I fucked up, but I couldn't listen to that woman speak to her like that."

"Listen, I get it, but Lucía isn't yours to defend. She's ours to protect because we're getting paid to do so and it's a favour for our Queen. You're not her knight in shining fucking armour."

"I know that. I was just trying to be a decent fucking person, that's all."

Bás looked at him, his head tilted slightly before he nodded once. "It better be."

Reaper wanted to leave to speak to Lucía and see if she was okay, but he had to bide his time and suffer through the rest of the evening until she was ready to retire. Focused on watching her as she chatted with Valentina and her sister, he didn't hear the Queen come up to him until she was almost beside him.

He dipped his head. "Your Majesty."

He could see the resemblance between the Queen and her daughters. Perhaps she was a little more petite in stature, but her head was held high on an elegant neck and there was a grace and class about her that he knew wasn't faked or put on. She was the real deal, reminding him very much of their own Queen Lydia. Not so much in looks but in her regal bearing.

"I've been waiting for a long time for someone to stand up for my daughter. I had hoped it would be her, but my youngest child is a peacemaker, always has been. Tonight, you shone a light on others' treatment of her and it forced my husband to speak out."

Reaper looked across at Lucía who glanced up at that moment, their eyes locking, and he felt a tug in his belly as if an invisible string was pulling him toward her. He knew he had to cut it, or they'd both end up hurt.

The attraction he felt for her was too strong and yet he knew as sure as he stood there that he wouldn't walk away and leave her protection to someone else. She was his and that was about as fucked up as this could get.

"I should have kept quiet. This isn't my place and she's not mine to fight for." He didn't know why he was admitting that to the Queen and mother of the woman who'd him tied up in knots.

"Perhaps."

Reaper turned his attention back to the Queen to find her watching him watch Lucía. "May I ask you a question?"

"You may, but I don't promise to answer."

"Why didn't anyone else speak up for her?"

The Queen sighed and went silent for a moment, and he wondered if he'd pushed his luck too far before she looked him in the eye. "In this family, it's imperative that you learn to stand up for yourself. My husband and I never wanted to fight her battles for her knowing that one day she'd need to fight her own. We needed her to have the backbone to do it."

"Believe me, Lucía has more backbone than anyone I know. I've been on the receiving end of it."

The Queen laughed, bringing the adoring gaze of her husband to them. "She does everywhere except here. For some reason, when she's home, she tries to be who she thinks she should be, not who she really is inside. I'm hoping that after tonight she learns that we love her for who she is, not what she should be. Lucía is perfect as she is, and if she showed her true self to the world there'd be no doubt who the Princess of the people would be."

"I hope so too."

"And if not, I know she has people around her who will show her the way." Her glance at Valentina and Bás confirmed what she meant.

"She does."

The Queen touched his arm and leaned in close. "Look after my daughter, Mr Carson. Be who she needs you to be, not what you think you should be to her."

On that she glided towards her husband, leaving Reaper more confused than ever. She seemed to think there was more going on than there was. Or had she seen something he couldn't? He didn't know but what he did see was that for the first time since arriving home, Lucía was wearing a genuine smile and the tenseness in her shoulders had eased.

CHAPTER 10

Justice had avoided her last night, hanging back as Valentina checked her rooms and said goodnight. Lucía wasn't sure how she'd felt about his outburst at dinner but this morning she felt good and a little sheepish. He shouldn't have had to do it and she realised she was in part to blame for what she'd allowed to happen.

Bouncing out of bed, she set the power on the coffee pot and headed for the shower. Today would be a good day because she got to catch up with some of her charity workers and look in on them and see how things were going.

As she showered it was hard to forget the image of Justice in just his towel and her body ached with arousal remembering his hard ridges and plains. Her battery-operated boyfriend had done nothing to ease the ache. She regretted letting it go so long without finding a lover, but her position hardly made that easy. Perhaps her long abstinence explained her ridiculous attraction to Justice Carson.

Dressing in dark green trousers and a cream blouse with a round neck and a loose bow, she blow-dried her hair so it lay in waves around her shoulders. She'd be wearing it up for the ball that night, so it didn't matter if it got blown around. Adding a light layer of make-up, she finished her coffee and the fruit that had been delivered while she was in the shower.

Knowing Justice was outside her door waiting for her gave her a funny butterfly feeling in her tummy, and she rushed to brush her teeth and put on her lip gloss before taking a second to calm her breathing. It wouldn't do for him to know how much he affected her. They'd only known each other just over a week, and this wasn't some whirlwind romance but a man doing his job. Lucía had to keep reminding herself of that, or she'd get swept away by the tidal wave of whatever this was.

Opening the door, she saw him turn to her, the ends of his blond hair curling over the collar of his navy suit. "Good morning, Princess Lucía. Are you ready to go?"

"Yes, I am. Is Valentina coming with us?" Lucía had gotten on well with the woman but today she hoped it was just the two of them.

"Valentina is taking care of some things here at the Palace but if you'd like her to come, I can find her and ask her to attend."

The formal way he was speaking to her made her frown. "Justice!"

His brows rose as he turned from walking her down the stairs, his body just in front as if trying to protect her, from what, she didn't know. "Yes, Princess?"

"Cut that shit out."

He didn't answer but his jaw flexed as he resumed his route, ushering her toward the car he'd drive her around in all day. Opening the door, he waited for her to get in before closing it. She watched him walk around to the driver's side and slide in, his scent filling the car and mixing with the leather from the upholstery, making it her new favourite smell.

As he drove away, he caught her eyes in the rear-view mirror. "So, what crawled up your ass this morning, Lucía?"

She smiled, relieved that the man she'd spent the last week with had returned. "Nothing. I just don't want the bowing and scraping I get from others from you. I need you to be you, like we were at home."

It wasn't lost on her how she referred to her cottage as home.

"I understand that and when we're alone, I'll be my usual uncouth self, but when people are around, I need to do this right. I've already pushed my luck speaking out as I did last night. I don't regret it, but I don't need to give the King another reason to fire me either."

"I understand and thank you for what you did. I'm ashamed and embarrassed that you had to do it and that I wasn't brave enough to stand up for myself. I've learned a lot about who I am this last week."

A growl came from the front seat, and he looked pissed as he caught her eyes in the mirror. "You have fuck all to be ashamed about. You did nothing wrong. The idiots who don't see you for the amazing person you are should be the ones feeling ashamed."

Lucía smiled, her gaze moving from the vista speeding past to his eyes in the mirror. "You think I'm amazing?"

Justice shook his head, but she caught the twitch of his lips. "Don't get excited, angel. I think Vegemite is amazing too."

Lucía wrinkled her nose in disgust, making him laugh. The deep, masculine sound of it made her squeeze her knees together as a bolt of lust hit her between her legs.

Arriving at the centre where Books for All was located, she smiled at seeing a line of children and volunteers waiting for her, smiles wreathed on their faces. Waiting for Justice to open the door, she took his offered hand as she stepped out, the zing of electricity between them when they touched seeming to grow with each day. Lucía snatched her hand back on an indrawn breath, her eyes shot towards his face and saw he was as affected as she was but was obviously better at hiding it.

"Princess Lucía, how wonderful to see you again."

Snapping out of her desire filled stupor, she turned her smile on Carlotta who ran the charity. "It's so wonderful to be back."

She was led inside and spent the next few hours going over what they'd achieved so far this year and what the plan was for the winter drive. She chatted with the staff, the volunteers, and some of the families who'd benefitted from the drive. She took several photos as well in the hopes she could use some of them for promotional work. She also chatted with the new leader of the Dyslexia programme they were running to try and encourage children with dyslexia to enjoy the written word. The whole time she could feel Justice's presence beside her, his constant nearness was driving her both crazy and making her want him closer still.

He smiled at the children and greeted the parents with a friendly demeanour while making sure nobody got closer than he was happy with.

Over lunch made by some of the parents, she asked what she could do to help.

"We need more money and to get the word out. The new programme is great, but we need qualified people to implement the changes."

Lucía moved her plate aside and crossed her legs. "How about a Christmas Ball? I could ask my father if he'd host it at the Palace."

She felt Justice bend close to her ear from his place behind her chair, his breath tickling her neck as he spoke. "Angel, you won't be here at Christmas. You'll be overseas."

"Oh yes, that's right. I won't be here, but I could ask my mother. She loves this kind of thing, and I wouldn't be the draw anyway if I can get the King and Queen to attend."

"It's a lovely idea, Princess Lucía, but we'd dearly love you to be there."

Lucía shivered as Justice bent down low again, so he could speak to her. "How about a Valentine's Ball?"

Lucía tried to focus on his words, not on how he was making her feel like the air was depleted, all lightheaded and giddy. "Yes, a Valentine's Ball would be perfect."

"But how would we raise money from it?"

Lucía concentrated on Carlotta and what she was saying, not the man whose presence behind her was so deliciously distracting. "We could charge for tickets and have an auction with all proceeds going to this charity."

Carlotta looked down pursing her lips. "But you'd be there?"

"Yes, I'd absolutely be there. I wouldn't miss it."

"That would be wonderful. Most of the parents are only involved because of you."

"Because of me?"

"Why, yes. They adore you and they come for you, not anyone else."

Pleasure bloomed in her chest at the thought that she was making a real difference here, not just her name but her as a person. "That's very kind of you to say." Lucía frowned. "How about we do something small in January just for the families and I can attend that as well?" She turned to Justice who was looking intense and gorgeous. "Is that possible?"

"We can make it work."

After another thirty minutes, she knew it was time to move on to the next charity, which was a children's charity that helped orphans of migrant parents find homes. Over her time as a war photographer, she'd seen so many displaced children with nothing and each time it broke her heart. It was the reason she set this charity up, to help bring some hope to those innocents who'd done nothing more than be born.

Once in the car, she began to look through some of the images she'd taken from the morning, her camera a near-constant part of her now and smiled at one of Justice surrounded by some of the mothers, a grin on his face as he looked at her and the camera.

As she went through them, she almost missed it but something made her flick back and there, clear as day in the background, was Felix. Her gasp drew Justice's attention.

His whole body went alert as he glanced around him and then back at her through the rear-view mirror. "What's wrong?"

"Felix is in this picture I took of the children!"

"What? Are you sure?"

Lucía glared at the back of his head. "Yes, I'm sure."

Seconds later Justice was on the phone and turning the car around in the road. "Bás, it's me. I need you to find Felix and have him brought in so I can question him. He was hanging around the Books for All charity headquarters and Lucía caught him on camera."

She couldn't hear the other side of the conversation, but she got the gist of it as Justice hung up.

"Bás is going to find Felix and have him secured. Valentina is heading our way as backup."

"Is that necessary?"

Justice glared at her, all the heat in his eyes that of fury now and she had a feeling he was blaming himself for not spotting Felix.

Sitting back in her seat she sighed as they sped back towards the Palace. "Okay, I get it."

ABOUT A MILE out from the city Justice swore as he glanced in his mirrors. "We have a tail. I need you to hold on, angel, this might get a bit bumpy."

Lucía turned, spotting the black Audi barrelling towards them at speed. "Wait, that's Felix's car."

"Are you sure?"

"Yes, he gloats about it all the time."

Justice went quiet as if he was summing up the plan of action he'd take next and running through the outcomes. "I'm heading back to the Palace. I'm not taking any chances with you."

As she went to answer, an explosion lit the afternoon, and she was thrown around as the car went flying, the seat belt the only thing keeping her in place. Screams and shouts sounded as she heard her name being called, lights flashed as pain lashed through her shoulder. She caught sight of Justice as he held on as best he could with glass shattering around them both before the car came to stop right side up in the middle of the road.

Stunned, she looked around, wincing as pain pierced her skull.

Lifting a hand she touched her head and found her fingers covered in blood. She could hardly hear a thing as her ears rang with the tinny, muffled sounds from the crash.

"Lucía!"

Looking up she saw Justice looking at her anxiously as he tried to get free of the seat belt that had most likely saved his life. He had a huge gash on his forehead and blood was dripping down his face.

"Justice, are you okay?"

"Yeah. We need to get out of here quick. I don't know how stable the car is or if another attack is coming."

Her hands were shaking as she tried to disengage the seat belt, but it was jammed. The sounds of sirens in the distance were a soothing reminder that help was coming as she tried to stop the panic building in her chest. A hand on her shoulder made her jump but when she looked up, relief and a sense of security swept through her making her lightheaded. Justice was somehow out of the car and beside her, having pulled the door open without her realising it in her panic-induced cloud.

"Let me take a look."

Reaching over, he tried to unclip the belt and when it didn't work, he used a knife from his pocket and cut through the harness holding her captive.

"Just breathe, angel. It's okay, you're going to be fine."

Her eyes on him she tried to match her breathing to his, copying his regular deep in and out breaths until the light-headedness began to ease.

"That's my girl, just keep breathing."

"I think my arm is broken and it hurts when I breathe."

"The ambulance is here and we're going to get you fixed up, angel. Just hold on, okay?"

"Okay."

Justice went to move away but she gripped his hand harder. "Don't leave me."

He crouched so she could see his face. She winced at the state of him as blood oozed slowly from his head and yet he looked calm, in control, and she was falling apart.

Tears pricked her eyes and she fought them back. "I'm sorry, I'm being silly."

His hand on her knee tightened, getting her attention and she looked back to see his stern face, soften. "I'm not leaving you, but I need to go around the other side and give the crew room to work. They need to check you over before they can move you."

Lucía nodded, the movement making her wince as the sound of onlookers and first responders dimmed. For the next thirty minutes, Justice held her hand while they checked her over, refusing care for himself until she was safely in the ambulance with Valentina by her side. As they did the final checks on her, he stepped into the ambulance, swapping places with Val. They exchanged a few words, which seemed intense but the drugs they'd given her for the pain were kicking in and everything was becoming a blur until finally she couldn't feel or hear anything.

CHAPTER 11

Reaper was pacing outside the room where they'd rushed Lucía to for tests after her arrival at the hospital. They weren't going to let him ride with her in the ambulance until the King had confirmed he was her bodyguard. The entire scene had been swarming with the royal security by the time they left but his only concern had been Lucía.

When he'd seen her bleeding and in pain, it had done something to him. His heart had cracked, and a thirst for vengeance for the person who'd done it had swelled up in him like a tsunami.

"What the hell happened?"

Reaper looked as Bás and Valentina approached, stopping mid-stride. "Is Felix dead?"

After the initial impact, he'd known they hadn't been the target. Felix's Audi had been hit by an RPG, the force from the explosion sending their car flying and injuring Lucía.

"Yes. It was just confirmed he died at the scene."

Reaper thrust his fingers through his hair in frustration something bigger was going on here and he didn't fucking like it one bit.

Val stepped closer putting a hand on his arm to still his movements. "How is Princess Lucía?"

He shook her off, he needed to keep moving to stop the image of her mangled dead body from going through his brain on a loop. "The doctors are with her now, but they think she'll be fine." He glanced up as two men walked down the corridor. They were tall and built, and the way they scanned the hallway for danger suggested they had military training. He didn't know them, but he guessed they were royal security.

Reaching them they stopped, and the larger man, with dark hair and a square jaw looked him up and down. "I'm Franco Santini, Head of Security at the Palace. You may go. I'm here to watch Princess Lucía myself."

Reaper clenched his jaw, his teeth almost ground to dust as he tried not to respond emotionally. The fist at his side flexed with an itch to punch this smug fucker in the face though. "Well, I don't take orders from you. Princess Lucía is mine to protect, so you can just turn around and run back to wherever it is you've been hiding all week."

Reaper could see the way the other man's eye twitched in anger at his authority being challenged and didn't give a fuck. Out of the corner of his eye, he saw the other man move as Bás flanked him, having his back, as did Val as she moved in closer.

Perhaps stepping up to this man now was a bad move but he wouldn't leave Lucía with anyone but him or one of his team, and the vibe he was getting off this guy was nothing but bad news.

"I've been busy."

"Yeah, while you've been busy people have been murdered, and the entire security of the Spanish Royal family has been compromised. I suggest you get your house in order and leave the Princess to me."

"You have no authority here."

Reaper stepped up so he was right in Santini's face, the green flecks in his eyes visible. "I couldn't give a flying fuck what you think.

I was told by the King himself to protect his daughter and that's what I'll do until he either tells me to leave or they drag my dead body from her side."

Santini looked him up and down with disgust, his lip curling, sweat dripping down his temple, and Reaper knew he'd just made another enemy to add to the growing list.

"That can be arranged."

"Bring it on but stay the hell away from Lucía or I'll make it my life's work to make you regret ever meeting me."

Santini's smug grin returned. "Hm, it seems our mutual friend is correct about you being hot-headed."

Reaper had a feeling he wasn't going to like whatever Santini said next, but he took the bait anyway. "Mutual friend?"

Santini leaned in close so only he could hear. "Playboy says hello."

White-hot anger made his vision go red and it took every ounce of control he'd ever had not to launch himself at Santini and demand answers, but he knew that was exactly what he wanted him to do. "He was never a friend. He's nothing more than a piece of shit who gets Daddy to clear up the mess he leaves behind."

"Hm, he said you'd say that, so he said to check your email."

Before Reaper could respond, the King was walking down the corridor of the hospital with his entourage, including the Queen, Princess Maria, and her husband. Guards flanked them on all sides, but it still made his teeth grind to see Santini position himself close to the Monarch.

"Your Majesty." Bás and Reaper dropped into a bow in deference to the King and the barely contained fury on his face.

"How is my daughter?"

"They're with her now, but she was talking and coherent until they gave her pain relief."

"I'll go and speak to the doctors, Father." Maria gave him a small smile and slipped into the room with her mother behind her, the door closing before he could get a good look inside to see that Lucía was, in fact, okay.

"How did this happen?"

"We haven't got the full details yet, but we believe an RPG hit Felix's car. The force of the blast launched our vehicle into the air."

"Felix was fired yesterday after we discussed his behaviour." The King stood tall, his bearing very much that of the leader he was. "Why was he following you?"

"That we don't know but we have our best analyst going through the footage now to see if we can glean any information."

"I want a report on my desk first thing tomorrow." His eyes moved to Bás before returning to Reaper, challenge and warning in the powerful man's eyes. "If you're not up to the task of protecting my daughter and keeping her safe then please tell me now so I can find someone who *is* capable."

His pride bruised by the words which he knew in his heart were warranted, Reaper straightened. "She's safe with me. Now I know the true extent of the threat, I'll take measures to ensure her safety."

King Juan looked at him and then his son-in-law, who nodded slightly.

Santini smirked thinking he'd won this round, but he was about to find out that when someone poked at wounds as old and raw as he had, then they were likely to get caught in the crossfire.

"Fine. Don't make me regret this."

"I won't, and, sir, if I may ask, can we meet privately first thing to discuss the report?"

Reaper saw the look pass between the two security specialists and knew that Val and Bás were taking in every nuance too.

"I'll arrange it myself."

Santini puffed up his chest. "Sir, I really must object. You know very little about these people."

The King turned on his head of security, giving him a look that would reduce most men to a weeping mess. "I suggest you do your job and find out why there are so many holes in my security, or you'll be looking for a new job come morning and will be objecting to nothing."

Santini nodded, his jaw rigid with anger at being taken down like that in front of them and his men.

"Now if you'll excuse me, I need to check on my family." He glanced to Santini. "You may head back to the Palace. Your men and these people will ensure me and my family get home safely."

Reaper nodded as Santini walked away with his man, the two muttering low but the conversation was obviously intense. King Juan and Lucas headed in to see Lucía, and Reaper was once again reminded who he was to her. He had no rights to her so why did he have to fight the urge to push past them all and hold her in his arms until he was sure she was okay?

Bás glanced down the corridor where Santini had gone. "We need to figure this out fast. There's way more going on here than we realised at first."

"Yeah, there is, and he mentioned something I need Watchdog to look into. He said we have a mutual friend in Playboy."

"The man from your old team?"

Val looked confused as she glanced between them, her hand fidgeting at her side as if she was missing her dogs, who were usually a constant at her side.

"Yes. Have Watchdog see if there's a link between Santini and Playboy and Chess, and do a deep dive into Santini and his men. He's as crooked as a dog's hind leg and I'd bet money that you'll find something in his background that the King's team didn't."

Val folded her arms over her chest, her hip cocked. "What about Felix?"

"Felix knew something, and he certainly didn't like Lucía, but I don't believe he's capable of this."

Reaper rubbed his head, a headache pounding where his head had hit the steering wheel.

Val laid a hand on his arm. "You should get some rest."

He gave her a wan smile. "I will when the Princess is back home and safe."

The smile she gave him showed she understood but there was a warning in her brown eyes too, and he knew she saw through him. To what, he had no clue because his feelings for the Princess were becoming more complex than he could unravel.

A commotion inside the room had him tensing, his hand on the door handle before he could register his movement. The scene that greeted him almost made him smile but he fought the urge as all eyes came to him.

"Justice, tell my father I'm okay!"

Lucía was sitting up in bed, a white hospital gown covering her body, her arm in a sling, and an IV in her arm as she argued with her father and the doctors.

"Ah," he stepped in and closed the door leaving Bás and Val to guard the door, "I'm not sure I'm qualified to overrule the King or a doctor."

Lucía huffed out a breath and glared at him as if he'd betrayed her before looking at her father again. The family dynamic and closeness was easy to see in this setting with emotions running high. They'd pulled together, tightened the circle, and he could see the love between them all and it made him miss his own family so much more.

"The doctor says my ribs are only cracked and my shoulder dislocation will heal with rest."

The King looked at the doctor who seemed to shrink under his gaze, the King, normally amiable and loved, was a dangerous lion protecting his cub right now. "And you'll stake your career on this?"

The man nodded, his glasses wobbling on his nose as he did. "If the Princess does as I've said she'll heal with no lasting repercussions. Her scans show no head trauma and she didn't lose consciousness. She'll need to rest and take it easy for a week or two and no lifting with that arm for six weeks."

Lucía gaped. "Six weeks!"

"Hush, mi hija." The King's voice was more indulgent now. "We'll take you home and have you resting in your room as long as you promise to behave."

Reaper watched her lips purse into a sexy pout which he shouldn't be finding sexy.

"Fine."

"Arrange it."

The King looked at him and lifted his chin to tell him to leave as he followed Reaper back into the corridor.

Once it was just the four of them, the three Shadow operatives and the King, he spoke. "Your Majesty, I believe I have an idea that will allow the Princess to heal in peace without the risk of her attacker knowing where she is."

Reaper hadn't discussed this with anyone yet. The idea had only come to him on a whim, but the more he thought about it the more he realised it was the best option.

"I'm listening."

"I'll take the Princess to my home in Australia. It's remote, her profile isn't as high there, and I have family around who will help care for her." He glanced at Bás. "If Bás will allow Valentina and two other operatives to accompany me, we'll have backup should we need it, but I don't think we will. Princess Lucía can heal in peace before she moves on to her assignment if that's what she still wants to do. It will also give us time to look into everything that's happening here and the threats that were made toward the Princess."

King Juan looked at Bás. "You agree?"

Bás at once nodded. "I do and I can make it work if I can have twenty-four hours to arrange it."

With a nod, the King greenlit his plans. Reaper knew what he was planning was the right thing to do for her safety. He just had to keep her at a distance so he didn't fall for her harder than he already had.

CHAPTER 12

"ARE YOU SURE YOUR FAMILY WON'T MIND ME JUST TURNING UP LIKE THIS?" Lucía had been fretting for the last half an hour as the flight taking them across the ocean from Spain to Australia got closer to its destination.

Justice glanced across at her from where he was sitting working on his laptop. His blue eyes scanned her face as he had since the accident two days ago as if cataloguing her injuries and again, she saw the regret and the blame he was placing on himself.

"My family is excited to meet you and you're going to love them."

Lucía smiled as she saw the genuine love and affection he felt for his family pass across his face. Leaving her own family 24 hours earlier had been hard but after everything that had happened, she knew it was the right thing. Only her father and sister knew where she was headed as Justice was concerned about a leak inside the Palace. Having postponed the ball and moved it to Valentine's Day, she'd persuaded her mother to incorporate her charity into it and she'd agreed, saying she'd call Carlotta and arrange it.

Her love for her mother and her admiration of her kindness to others only made her wonder more about Justice's family. The people who'd agreed without question to host a Princess in trouble. "Tell me about them."

Justice leaned back in his seat. "Well, my mum's name is Elodie, and she works for a local law firm as a personal assistant. She lives in the house we grew up in and loves to cook and garden but hates the heat, so normally tends her garden in the early morning before the sun gets a hold. Caleb is my younger brother and he and his husband John are both successful architects, with a beachfront home on the Gold Coast. They have two children. Melody, who's named after my mum, is three, and Jake is four."

"You sound close."

Justice sat back, his face and posture reflective as if he was far away. "We are but I don't see them as much as I'd like."

"So how come you took this job? You clearly love your family, and the UK is very far away."

She could practically see the walls come down as she asked the question and knew he wasn't going to tell her anything, but he was wrong, his clamming up told her more than he probably wanted.

"You can freshen up in the bathroom before you land if you want. Val can help you."

Sighing, Lucía nodded and stood awkwardly as he grabbed her upper arm to steady her. The electricity zinged through her body at his touch and she gasped, her eyes shooting to his and seeing the feelings mirrored in his. They stayed locked in a bubble of awareness, just the two of them for a moment. She couldn't decide if she wanted him to give in and kiss her and show her how good she knew it would be between them or step away and spare herself the regret when they had to separate.

Val saved them from making a choice. "Need some help cleaning up?" Her smile was radiant as she looked between them, clearly ignoring the undercurrent of sexual tension.

"Yes, please. It's tricky getting my arms up with my ribs and my shoulder so limited."

"No problem. That's what I'm here for."

Lucía was mostly glad she was there. Except for now when what she really wanted to do was drag Justice into the bedroom at the back of the plane and see if the mile high club was all it was cracked up to be.

Along with Valentina, Bishop and Hurricane had also joined them. Hurricane was a beast of a man who looked like he lifted small cars for sport. He had black skin the colour of polished ebony and was tall, probably six foot five at least. His biceps, which were bigger than her thigh, made him seem imposing. Yet his eyes were gentle and he smiled a lot, making him feel safe, when if he worked for this team, he was most likely as deadly as the rest of them.

Bishop was different. He was smaller framed, still tall but his strength was leaner, like Justice. He had dark hair with a scar on his cheekbone and brown eyes but he was quiet, watchful as if he'd been trained to blend in and go unnoticed. His British accent had a northern roundness to it, and she expected a lot of people underestimated him and lived to regret it.

Valentina was now the only other woman on the team, and she'd told her she'd be having her dogs shipped to her and they'd be allowed to quarantine where they were staying for ten days as they were service dogs.

It was easy to hear in her voice how much she missed them and Lucía couldn't wait to meet them, having always wanted a pet and never having a dog that was just a family pet. The ones that belong to the Palace Guard weren't friendly or pets. While she knew that was still true with these animals, she'd also heard how one of the other team member's six-year-old daughter was helping to train them and figured they couldn't be too ferocious in that case.

Having changed into a white sleeveless shirt, making it easier to get in and out of, and conscious of the heat this time of year as Australia went into their summer, she added a cotton skirt in yellow, and flat tan-coloured sandals.

Her hair was in a long ponytail off her neck, and she touched up her make-up as best she could, knowing she was lucky to have such good skin, just the bruises and the dark circles under her eyes needed covering.

Heading back to her seat she saw Justice talking to Hurricane and Bishop. All three men looked up when she entered, and she knew whatever they were talking about had been about her. An awareness flickered in Justice's eyes as he looked at her before he looked away, breaking the connection.

"He's a heartbreaker."

Lucía turned, seeing Val had come up behind her and caught the exchange. Her cheeks flamed as she sat and busied herself with her seat belt, Valentina eventually having to help her before taking a seat opposite where Justice had been sitting on take-off.

"I have no intention of finding out." Her words felt brittle even to her own ears and she regretted taking her frustrations out on the woman who'd shown her nothing but kindness. "I'm sorry."

"No, it's okay. I do tend to poke my nose in when I shouldn't. I think it comes from having a brother who was emotionally stunted by his experience with the woman he loved."

Intrigued now, Lucía leaned forward. "Emotionally stunted?"

Val's lips quirked. "Yeah, he was left at the altar by the love of his life and it made him a little jaded about love."

"Oh no, how awful for him. I can't imagine doing that to someone."

"He's fine now. Happily married to the same woman actually, so it all worked out."

Lucía couldn't imagine being so forgiving. "He must love her very much."

"He does. He adores her and she adores him. Their story is a complex one I won't go into but suffice to say, it all worked out how it should have."

"What about you? Any man on the horizon?"

Valentina laughed causing the three men to look over, frowns on their handsome faces. "No, this job doesn't allow much time for finding love and it's not what I need right now."

"Really? I was sure I saw a spark between you and Bás."

Val's head shot up, her eyes wide with surprise and maybe a little hope or perhaps panic. "God, no. He and I are friends, that's all. And in any case, we work together, and work relationships are strictly prohibited in this job."

"Shame. You two would be great together."

"So back to what I was saying earlier and changing the subject in a not-so-subtle fashion, Reaper is a heartbreaker, but he looks at you differently than I've seen him look at anyone before. I've seen the sparks. This can only end in heartbreak for you both, Princess Lucía, so please be careful. I'd hate to see either of you hurt."

Lucía didn't want to lash out or hurt this woman, so she was careful with her words. "I appreciate your concern but there really is nothing to be worried about."

Valentina regarded her as if knowing the lie she told but merely nodded and left her to her own thoughts as the flight began its descent.

Butterflies fluttered in her tummy and her eyes danced across the cabin to Justice. She had no idea what it was about him that made her ache, made her want to be someone different just so they could see what could be between them, but it was a fool's game. She was who she was and so was he, and a relationship between them would never work.

Once the plane had taxied to a stop and they'd disembarked, she was rushed out of the door toward a waiting car that already had Bishop behind the wheel. His nod as she got in made her feel secure, but not as safe as the man who sat beside her, his eyes on the road around them, tension in his body as if he was coiled for a battle that she couldn't see.

"Is everything alright?"

His gaze came to hers and the instant attraction seemed to fill the car, so it felt like it was just the two of them. His hand resting on his leg moved a fraction and his little finger brushed her thigh like a whisper. She shivered with desire, her eyes closing as if too heavy to stay open.

"Everything will be fine when I have you safe at my home."

The idea of being in his space surrounded by the people he loved the most gave her a funny feeling in her tummy she couldn't explain. "I'm excited to meet your family but also a little nervous."

"Nervous? Why would you be nervous? You're a Princess for goodness' sake."

"Maybe but that doesn't mean I don't feel the same things as other people. I once got so star struck meeting Tom Cruise at a premiere that I could hardly speak. He must have thought I was a complete dolt."

Justice's husky laugh warmed her belly and made her itch to make him do it again, this severe protector who'd seen more than he'd ever let on.

"I doubt it, darlin'. He was probably trying to figure out how to get you into his bed."

Lucía blushed and shook her head, not wanting to admit that although Tom had been a complete gentleman, his co-star had indeed tried to get her alone. "My point is I'm human."

His eyes swept over her body deliciously slowly. "Oh, I'm aware."

Her body warmed despite the air conditioning moving about the car. She knew he saw the way he affected her when he winked, an arrogant sexy move that made her want to crawl into his lap and take what she needed from him. Although she couldn't see him allowing that. She had a feeling he'd be in charge of whatever happened between them, and her traitorous body wanted it all.

CHAPTER 13

As they drew up to his mother's home with Hurricane and Valentina following in a car behind them, Reaper bit back a sigh, but it wasn't one of anger, more annoyance. His brother's favoured hire car, a Mercedes was sitting in the drive alongside his mother's more modest KIA. He'd half expected his brother to show up when he'd heard he was home but had hoped for a day to get Lucía settled before he bombarded her with his family. Much as he loved them, they could be a lot.

As the car drew to a halt, the front door opened and his mother, looking as if she hadn't aged a day, was running towards him, her arms open wide. Exiting the car with a grin, he caught his mum in his arms and lifted her feet off the ground for a hug.

"Oh, my boy, it's so good to have you home."

Guilt swirled through him at her words, though no censure was intended. He loved his family, and he knew they struggled with him being so far away. Yet he couldn't explain to them the need for distance to keep fighting evil in the only way he knew how. He wasn't even sure he understood it himself. "Missed you, Mum."

As he put her down, keeping his arm around her shoulders, her head barely touching his chest, he turned to Lucía, who'd come to stand beside him. Her smile held nerves and warmth and once again it was like a sucker punch to the gut. She was more than just beautiful on the outside, her personality exuded kindness and joy and he was no more immune than anyone else. "Mum, this is Princess Lucía."

His mum went to give a curtsey and Lucía reached out a hand to stop her. "Please, while I'm here, I'm Lucía, a friend of your son's and you're very kind to offer me a place in your home."

His lips twitched, his heart warming with the way she was treating his mother.

"It's a pleasure to meet you and Justice's friends are always welcome in my home." His mum clapped her hands, going into organiser mode with the flip of an invisible switch. "Come in out of this heat and let's get you settled."

Justice held out a hand for Lucía to follow his mother, a smile on his face as some of the tension he'd been feeling melted away.

Val, Hurricane, and Bishop would be staying in Cairns but not at the house. Bás had decided that too many new people in the neighbourhood, would make it more likely they'd stand out, so they'd be a few streets away in a rental and could get to them in minutes if needed. He agreed it was the best option and while that was going on, Watchdog, Val, Hurricane, and Bishop would continue to investigate, Bishop being the one with the most helpful contacts. His years as an MI5 spy had given him intelligence and knowledge about people he could leverage, and he wasn't shy about doing it the hard way if the job warranted it.

Looking around his family home, he was hit by a wave of nostalgia. For years he'd convinced himself that there were no happy memories here, but time and space had given him the distance to remember the good. His father had coloured so much of his childhood but in her own way, so had his mother, and it was those memories that he felt filling his mind now.

Laughter from the den on the left of the kitchen made him look up to see Caleb walking through the door, a large grin on his face.

"Justice, it's about time you got yourself home. We missed you, bro." Caleb was the same height as him, with the same hair and eye colour but he was slimmer, less muscled, leaner. While Justice lived in jeans or combat trousers when he wasn't forced into a suit, Caleb was like a walking fashion doll.

Justice hugged his brother and patted his back. "Looking good, Caleb."

Caleb ran his hand down his front with a flourish. "When do I look anything else?"

"How about at three in the morning when you've had one too many glasses of brandy?" John, his husband, said from the door with a chuckle, his eyes warm as they watched them both.

"Now don't go making me look bad in front of Princess Lucía."

Justice moved across to where Lucía was talking to his mum and caught her eye as he moved closer, his body drawn like a magnet to hers. He could practically feel the vibrations of her body as he closed in as if there was a frequency that only they could hear that their bodies responded to.

"Lucía, this is Caleb, my brother, and his husband John."

"It's a pleasure to meet you both."

"Oh my God, is that a Catherine Walker skirt?"

Justice looked at the simple yellow skirt she wore which somehow seemed to enrich the colour of her hair and just saw a nice skirt. Judging by his brother's excitement though, it was a designer he knew.

"It is. I just love her stuff."

Caleb wrapped his hand around Lucía's shoulder and ushered her towards the den, which led to the garden and the pool. He could hear Caleb and Lucía talking as he lifted his bag and glanced at his mother who was knocking up a feast for lunch.

"Is Lucía in the addition?"

"Yes, darling. I set everything up for her and you're in your old room. Caleb and John are headed back tonight."

"Oh." Disappointment rose in him at the thought of his brother and John, who was like a brother, leaving so soon.

John sipped a glass of wine, his lips twitching. "Oh, don't worry, we'll be back next weekend with the kids. That is if I can get Caleb to come home now he's found a woman after his own heart."

Laughter found his ears and he liked the sound of Lucía's sexy chuckle in his home. "She has that effect on everyone."

"Hmm, so I see."

Justice didn't respond to the loaded non-comment but picked up his bag and carried it to his room. Heading back to the hallway where Hurricane had left Lucía's belongings, he moved them through to the addition. It was a beautiful self-contained area of the house with its own kitchenette, bathroom, small living space, and bedroom. It had been built for his grandmother on his mother's side but she'd never gotten to use it before she died. The furniture was new, and the décor was elegant, having been chosen by Caleb with his mother's supervision so he didn't go too wild.

His bedroom was the other side of the wall so he was close in case she needed him, not that he thought she would. Lucía had stubbornly refused Val's offer to stay there and help her, insisting she'd be better used finding the people behind the attacks.

Leaving her bags, he closed the door and headed to his own room to call Bás. The decoration was plain navy bedding with white walls and a hardwood floor with a wooden dresser. He'd spent all his time outside, so he hadn't needed much. Still, it was strange to be back, and he found it was easy to fall into the family swing as if he'd never left.

Dialling the secure line, he waited.

"Yes?"

"We're here and secure. The team have gone to the safe house."

"Good, because we have a development."

"Oh?"

"Yeah, Watchdog got hacked."

Justice sat up straighter, his awareness pricked. "No way."

"Yes, way and he's pissed as hell."

Reaper could imagine he was, he prided himself on being un-hackable. "He know who did it?"

"No, but he's closing in on them."

"Was anything taken or compromised?"

"Not that we can see but be extra vigilant until we know for sure."

He walked to the patio door which led from his room to the side deck and the pool area at the back of the house. Lucía was sitting with Caleb and John, her face animated as she spoke, and the two were men enraptured just as much as he was by the remarkable woman. "You think this is connected?"

"I don't know but my gut says yes."

"Any location on Playboy or Chess yet?"

"No, nothing. All we know is they left the military two years ago and went dark. There was suspicion of a misconduct allegation but nothing on record, just rumours. Do you know his father is now the Minister for Defence in Australia?"

"Yes, I'd heard that, and I'm not surprised about Playboy or Chess. They're both nasty bastards. More so Playboy, but perhaps Chess just hides it better."

"I know and I know this is personal for you with them, but we need to find out why they're targeting the Princess. It can't be because of you, as you came to this after the first threat."

"No, that's not right. The first threat was the video."

Bás was silent for a beat. "We thought that was the case but apparently there was a threat sent to the Palace before that, which is the real reason the King came to us."

His blood was pumping faster through his veins now. He'd convinced himself the threat was coming from Playboy. He was certain it was him in the video and that the threat had been because of him. But if there'd been threats before then, it meant the Princess was in real danger and knew something she hadn't told him about or was unaware of.

"Does she know?"

"No, the King didn't want her to worry."

Reaper paced, anger burning through him at the danger she'd been put in because of secrets others were keeping. Had he known the threat had been sent there first, he never would've gone to Spain. "And Santini, is he the leak?"

"We think so but have nothing concrete to take to the King and he's being stubborn."

"What about Felix?"

"Watchdog was going through his phone but the hack happened and he needs to secure that first."

"Is it possible that's what they were looking for? There might be something on the phone they don't want us to see, and the hack is a smokescreen."

"It's possible. I might ask Will Granger to help us out or maybe Lopez."

Both men were on the same level as Watchdog with their hacking skills, but Watchdog outranked almost everyone on the planet in terms of how clever he was and it was to their benefit, but Lopez or Will would certainly be able to help. Both had the security clearance, Lopez worked for Eidolon the mother branch of Shadow, and Will was a part-owner.

"That's a good idea."

"Okay. Well stay frosty and I'll be in touch."

Bás hung up and Reaper smiled. Bás was another person who didn't bother with goodbyes and Reaper understood it. Since the day his grandfather had died when he was nineteen, he'd never said goodbye to another person he cared about, hating the finality of the words.

A knock sounded on his door, and he pulled it open to see Lucía looking hesitant but happy standing on the threshold. "Your mum said to find you and tell you lunch was ready."

Reaper stepped back, the urge to touch her was so potent his hand shook, so he clenched his fist to stop the feeling.

She stepped inside and he stepped further back to give her room that he didn't want to give. He wanted to touch her, feel her skin, and see if it was as soft as he imagined it to be.

"So, this is the young Justice Carson's bedroom."

He looked around seeing it through her eyes and the modest furniture and space. He shrugged. "Yep, this is me."

Her lips twitched into a smile that lit her face, the bruises marring her perfection making his blood boil. Without thought, he reached out to brush his fingers over the skin of her cheek, the bruise already beginning to fade from the horrid black to the hideous yellowy-green beneath her make-up. "Does it hurt?"

She shrugged and his eyes moved to the delicate curve of her shoulder. "Not too much."

His eyes moved over her, and he saw the way she shivered, the pulse in her throat beating in cadence with his own. "You're a tough one to resist, angel."

He could hear the gravel of desire in his own voice even as the noises from the rest of the house reached his ears and still, he couldn't seem to break the spell that came over him every time she was close. It was a bad thing for a man trying to protect her to be so distracted. He knew deep in his heart though nobody would protect her like he would, because in that second as her breath whispered out of her pouty lips, he knew he'd die for her.

"Then don't."

His control gone he hooked an arm around her waist and gently pulled her close, careful of her injuries as his lips found hers and she sighed into his kiss as if she'd been waiting for it all her life. He understood because to him it felt like he had. He'd never been so affected by a simple kiss, but the way she surrendered to him, her body softening and melding to his hard one, made it feel like so much more.

She tasted of strawberries and mint, so innocent and perfect he wanted to consume her, to own her in ways no other man ever had, and the thought shook him enough to make him pull away.

Her finger rose to his lips, her eyes dark and liquid as she watched him, and he knew he could drown in her expression right then. "Don't say you regret it, please."

He didn't regret it. The kiss had been beyond his expectations to the point he could spend all day just exploring her mouth and listening to the sounds she made in the back of her throat. "I wasn't going to. I was going to ask what you wanted to do about this thing between us because it isn't going away."

She tipped her head to the side, exposing her elegant throat and he wanted to feel the pulse there with his lips, to mark her perfect skin so every man knew she was his. But she wasn't and that was the hardest pill to swallow.

"While I'm here, I'm Lucía, not a Princess but a woman, so I propose we have a fling and get it out of our systems."

"You think you can get me out of your system, angel?" His words were said with a smirk, but he waited, his breath still in his lungs for her answer.

"I can if you can."

And there it was, the ultimate dilemma. He knew deep down that there was something different about Lucía for him and that once he'd tasted heaven, he'd never get her out of his system. Yet he nodded, knowing that he agreed to the impossible because not knowing the way she felt under him, over him, touching him, wasn't an option.

"So, a short-term fling that ends when we leave Australia and then we go back to bodyguard and principle? No harm, no broken hearts, no regrets?"

He tipped his head finding her eyes, needing to know she understood because from the start they'd never had a future but right now might be enough. It had to be.

"Yes. Let's treat this like a slice of time where I can be who I want to be, not who the world and everyone thinks I should be."

His lips found hers, as he spoke against them. "I think you're perfect no matter who you are, because inside here," he tapped a finger to her chest where her heart lay, "you're perfect as you are."

"Don't make me fall in love with you, Justice. It won't end well."

He frowned, not moving his lips from where they fluttered against hers. "I'm not trying to make you fall for me."

"Yeah, that's the problem."

Lifting on her toes she kissed him this time, sealing the deal they'd just made and promising things that made his body ache for her in a way he'd never felt before.

"Justice, get your butt in here and set the table. Just because you're the prodigal son doesn't mean you get out of chores."

Caleb appeared around the door his eyes twinkling, eyebrows waggling at the scene he found, and they both laughed.

"Come on, Princess. Let's go eat with my crazy family."

CHAPTER 14

THE MEAL ELODIE HAD PREPARED WAS WONDERFUL. CHICKEN PARMIGIANA with a green salad and bread rolls, followed by passionfruit pavlova. Sitting back, she tapped her stomach wishing her skirt had an elasticated waist. "Mrs Carson, that was fantastic. I don't think I can move, so you'll just need to roll me out of here."

Elodie laughed and it reminded her of how Justice had laughed with Valentina and Bishop on the flight over. "It's Elodie and I'm glad you liked it. Do you cook at all?"

She glanced at Justice, a smile twitching her lips as he watched her through sexy hooded eyes. "I do actually, and I have to confess that Justice showed me how to make your famous burgers, and they're the best burgers I've ever tasted."

Elodie blushed her hand patting her hair. "I'm lucky, both my boys can cook and iron. I never wanted to make them into men who had to rely on a woman to eat."

"Well, it seems like you did a wonderful job."

"Yes, but can Justice design a building to compete with the Sydney Opera house?" Caleb questioned, a natural sibling rivalry showing its head.

Justice threw a bread roll at his brother. "Can you shoot a terrorist from a mile away?"

Caleb threw it back, but Elodie's hand reached out to intercept the doughy projectile. "Boys, please behave. We have a guest and I'm sure she's not used to such juvenile behaviour." Her words were stern and Lucía had to hold her laughter in as both grown men dropped their heads.

"Sorry, Ma."

"Sorry, Mum."

"That's better. Now you two clean up this mess while I show Lucía her room."

Justice stood but dipped his head close, his hand resting on her shoulder, the skin there tingling from his touch and the silent promise in his eyes. "Will you be okay while I clean up?"

Her hand reached up and covered his hand as his thumb moved in small circles on her skin, the scene at once carnal and innocent. "Of course, your mother is wonderful."

Justice glanced at his mum, his face full of love. "Yeah, she is."

Not sure if they were keeping their relationship a secret, she was shocked when he dropped a kiss on her shoulder, her breath a gasp amongst the sound of the china being cleared from the table.

Straightening up, he winked as he began to stack the dishes up his forearm like a pro. He was such a contradiction. So tough and dangerous. She knew he'd killed people and seen horrible atrocities yet he retained his humour and love for life. That was the thing about her job, she'd seen the same things more than likely. At least enough that she'd begun to let those experiences change her.

She just couldn't be who her family needed. She felt a duty to give more, to do more, to make herself worthy of the family she'd been born into. The weight of it had been slowly suffocating her which was why she'd been so determined to do this six-month stint in the Middle East. To see if the places she'd photographed in the past had healed at all because she needed it to heal.

Yet as she sat there, the weight didn't feel so heavy, the pain of what she'd witnessed duller. The guilt that still weighed the same she could rationalise. If she'd stopped the attack she'd witnessed, the chances were she wouldn't have survived herself. It all seemed so long ago, and time had healed her a little, but here, in the beauty of this place, nothing seemed as dark.

"Now, my dear, let me show you the garden and your room and you can take a nap or shower if you want. For the next however long, this is your home and I expect you to treat it as such. Help yourself to whatever you need and if you can't find something, ask Justice and he will."

Lucía strolled around the large garden, admiring the pool, the water glinting in the light. She knew she'd be taking a dip in there as soon as she got the okay from the doctor Justice had secured for her follow up care. They chatted about the garden and Lucía asked the names of the different flowers as they walked. As they came around the side of the property, she saw two sliding doors and Elodie stopped outside the first.

"This is you." Elodie nodded towards the other door. "Justice is next door."

Pulling open the door, she let Lucía go first. The addition was beautiful and reminded her of her cottage in England. It had an open plan kitchenette and the living space had a television, two comfy chairs, and a two-seater couch facing the window to the back.

A bedroom was off the hallway beside the kitchen and had a full bathroom, and on the other side was a door that led into the interior hallway of the house. The décor was light and airy with touches of luxury here and there and she could see Caleb's hand all over. "This is beautiful."

Elodie clasped her hands together as she looked around a sad expression on her face. "Yes, it is. Caleb was the one who designed it and we had it built for my mother, but she died before she could use it."

She reached for Elodie's hand and squeezed, offering her comfort. "Oh, I'm so sorry."

She smiled as if pushing the memory away. "It's fine. It was a long time ago and my son learned of his love for designing from this very project, so it was meant to be in many ways."

"What about Justice? Did he always want to be in the military?" She found herself wanting to know more about the man she'd promised not to fall in love with, even as the sweet promise of sharing her body with him made her body electrify.

A faraway look crossed her face and she looked to be in another time, a not so happy one. "Justice wasn't really given a choice. My husband was military, and he was a high-ranking soldier. He assumed Justice would follow in his footsteps. My boy always wanted to please him so he did. But his heart was soft, and I know it cost him greatly. Even if he did turn out to be as good as he was, it took something from him. Every tour he went on he came home different, until one day it took it all. I knew when he left he needed to go to save himself."

Lucía felt her heart break for the boy without a choice and a willingness to do what he could to secure the love of his parent at any cost. Wasn't she trying to do the same thing when she allowed people to treat her as they had at the Palace?

"Well, he seems pretty good to me and I'm sure that's down to you."

"Everything good about me came from my mother. My father is a miserable piece of shit."

They both turned toward Justice's voice and his face was a mask of anger and pain. She wanted to go to him and soothe it away but stayed where she was standing. His mother patted her hand with a warm smile and walked toward her son. Reaching up, she kissed his cheek as he bent toward her, his eyes never leaving Lucía, the storm raging inside him barely contained. As his mother left, closing the door quietly behind her, she could barely breathe past the torrent of emotion swirling inside her.

Her mind and body were exhausted from the explosion, her

injuries, and the long flight yet all she could think about was this man in front of her and how he made her feel.

His eyes moved over her, intent on discovering all her secrets. "You're exhausted."

She went to argue, to deny his claims but at that second a wave of tiredness almost felled her and she swayed.

"Lie down and take a nap. You need to rest more if you want to heal quickly and for what I have planned, I need you healed, Lucía."

The wicked torment of longing for what he promised made her ache as he ushered her toward the bed, his hand on her back.

"Has anyone ever told you that you're bossy?"

His chuckle was warm, erasing the dark shadow the mention of his father had brought. "Yes, once or twice." He helped her remove her sandals, his fingers nimble and gentle as they brushed her skin. "Do you have anything to sleep in?"

Lucía nodded at her case. "Yes, in my case on the left-hand side."

A blush stained her cheeks as she saw him going through her things and she shook her head at her ridiculousness. She'd given herself to an affair with this man she was so attracted to and yet the thought of him touching her underwear made her blush.

"This?"

He held up a night slip and she nodded as he brought it to her.

"Stand up and I'll undo the button on your skirt so you can step out of it. I can do the buttons on your blouse, or I can ask my mother to come back in and help you."

"No!" Her shout of denial was out before she could temper it. "Don't leave me."

Justice nodded and helped her to stand again as he deftly undid the buttons and pushed the blouse from her shoulders, helping her unhook the fabric from her sling. His eyes remained on her face as he grasped her shoulders, turning her to face away from him. The heat of his body burned through her skin despite the cool breeze of the air conditioner.

When the fabric caught on her hips, she shimmied to make it

move and bumped back into him. The hiss of breath from him as he gripped her hips and the feel of the hard ridge of his erection against her ass made her moan involuntarily.

As she went to move, he gripped her tighter. "Be still, Lucía. I'm holding on by a fucking thread here."

The sense of power she felt at his words was one she'd never felt before and it empowered her to ignore the warning and turn in his arms. She knew the sling around her arm and the bruises on her skin should put a dent in how she felt but the way he was looking at her made her feel like the only woman in the world.

Reaching out she brushed her fingers over his tee where it met the waistband, inching it up so she could feel the warmth of his skin the spring of hair that led into his pants. "Take it off."

His eyes flared and he reached behind his head to grasp the neck, pulling the shirt up and over in one sexy move, before letting it drop to the floor.

Lucía let her eyes move over the dips and ridges of his body. The last time she'd seen him he'd been wet from the shower and had made her mouth water. Now her mouth was dry with need as she followed her eyes with her fingers, exploring his body and feeling his belly quiver beneath her touch. "You're so beautiful."

His chuckle was deep, smooth like a fine whisky. "Not sure if that bang on the head affected your eyes, angel, but there's only one beauty in this room and that's you."

Her eyes flashed to his and she shook her head. "No, you're the epitome of masculine beauty."

He stayed silent for a beat then he reached for her, lifting her in his arms and laying her on the bed. Stepping back, he slid the buckle of his belt free, the sound building anticipation in her blood before he lowered the zipper and removed his jeans. Her breath hitched as she looked at the hard line of his cock evident in the black boxers that did nothing to conceal his impressive length. His knee hit the bed between her legs and he sat back and looked his fill, a trail of goosebumps littering her skin from his gaze. His hand ran from between her breasts down her belly and over her thigh, and she arched her back desperate for release, her entire body pulsing.

"Please, Justice."

He didn't make her beg, instead, he dipped his head, pulling her nipple into his mouth, the lace of the bra a rough abrasion against her skin, adding to the intensity of pleasure. Her hands rested on his head, her body bucking as he laid the same claim on her other breast. He released her breast with a kiss that was drugging as his hand snaked beneath her back and flicked the clip on her bra before he drew the straps down her shoulders, his hands gentle as he released her arm and laid it on her belly leaving her free of the sling.

His eyes travelled over her, and she bit her bottom lip to bite back the moan at the sight of him looking at her like he might devour her, high slashes of colour across his cheeks. His hand ran over her skin, his lips following as he kissed and licked his way over her skin, her nipples tight buds of need as his fingers toyed with them and his teeth nibbled her inner thigh.

"Stop teasing me." Her voice was a growl and she felt him smile against her leg before he kissed her and sat back, pulling her underwear down her legs, his gaze on her bare pussy. His eyes were dark with need, she knew she was wet, the evidence of her desire for him glistening on her skin.

His eyes on her face, he ran a finger through her slit, gathering the evidence of her desire before sucking his finger into his mouth, his eyes closing in pleasure as she groaned and his growl filled the air. Then he was bending, lifting her hips with his forearms, and tucking a cushion beneath to support her, the thoughtful deed making tears sting the back of her eyes. His mouth then devoured her like a starving man. His tongue thrust into her as he licked and sucked her bundle of nerves.

A cry left her mouth, and she grabbed a cushion to stifle the sounds of pleasure she couldn't hold back. The climax hurtled towards her, legs shaking, body tensing, and she felt like she was on the precipice of something monumental, holding back fear that if she let go she'd explode into a thousand tiny pieces and never be the same again.

His mouth left her, and she groaned in despair as she threw the cushion to the side to glare at him. His eyes were intense as they watched her, the blue so deep like the ocean during a summer storm.

"Let go, angel. I won't let you fall. I'll never let you fall."

As his lips found her clit and he redoubled his effort. She trusted him, knowing without question that he'd catch her and that he'd honour his word. Just that knowledge was enough to push her over the edge where she stilled before falling, a million sensations flooding her body as it pulsed with pleasure like she'd never known before. Tiny aftershocks of her orgasm made her body jerk as he lifted his head and smiled. The wetness of her climax covered his chin and the sexy smirk made her heart skip a beat. He lowered her body to the bed and wiped his mouth with the back of his hand before crawling in beside her and rolling her to her side so her injured shoulder was on top.

Not sure what was happening she turned her head and he kissed her before she could speak. Her body languid and soft from the explosive climax she felt drugged by him, and a warm feeling of affection overwhelmed her.

Releasing her, he looked down at her before pressing another kiss to her lips as if he couldn't seem to stop from doing so. "Get some rest, angel."

Settling in behind her she felt the evidence of his need for her pressing into her back and made to move. He held her fast, his arm across her waist, the other he'd pushed beneath her neck, making his biceps her new favourite pillow.

She wiggled against him even as her eyes closed. "What about you?"

"Ignore it."

"That's kind of hard to do."

"Will you stop giving him attention, you're making it worse."

"Then let me take care of you."

His breath tickled her ear. "No, that was for you. You need to rest and get better before we take this further."

"That doesn't seem fair."

"I'll live."

She wriggled again and he groaned, grinding his hips against her ass to try and ease the ache. "You sure?"

"No, I might die, but if I do then at least I die in the knowledge that I did right by you. Now go to sleep."

Her body relaxed into his as he pulled the sheet over them both, his legs tangled with hers, the hair on his calves tickling her. As she felt sleep pull her under, she couldn't stop the smile from creasing her lips. Her body relaxed, her mind was clear of the flotsam of the last few weeks and she slept.

CHAPTER 15

THE SUN GLINTED OFF THE WATER AS REAPER PADDLED OUT TO SEA, THE SUN kissing his skin with warmth. The smell of salt filled his nose and filled him with a contentment he hadn't felt ever before. The last two weeks had been almost perfect. He'd spent their days showing Lucía the sights of Cairns. They'd been snorkelling in Palm Cove, visited the great barrier reef, had picnics, and walked and talked as if they'd known each other for years. Everything was easy between them, natural, and then there were the nights.

They hadn't had sex yet. He was conscious of her shoulder and ribs, and he didn't want to hurt her. They'd done most other things though. He'd found seeing her face contort with the beauty of her climax was his favourite thing to watch and had spent hours doing so.

"Come on, slowpoke."

Caleb was paddling up behind him, a glint of sibling rivalry in his eye that made Reaper grin. The reconnection with his family had given him great satisfaction and made him realise how much he missed them. For years he'd avoided coming home, where so many memories of the father he hated lived but being home now, he knew it wasn't the case. The love between him and his brother, mum, niece and nephew, and even John was the overriding feeling. He was grateful that Caleb and John had made the trip up from the Gold Coast again.

A splash of water hit his face and he glared at Caleb, whose face was alive with laughter. "Oh, it's on. I can beat your puny ass any day of the week and twice on Sundays."

"Put your money where your mouth is, bro."

Reaper grinned and began to paddle harder, the waves were perfect and as he waited for the perfect one to roll in, he relished the freedom of the sea. He missed it and yet this still felt like a holiday, not his real life.

As he began to paddle back to shore, chasing the wave and waiting for the perfect moment, the energy and zest for life he'd been missing filled him and he rode it into shore, a smile wreathed on his face that couldn't be torn away.

Jumping off his board he grinned at Caleb and high fived him. "Nice one."

"You, too. I thought perhaps land life had stolen your mojo."

Reaper laughed as his eyes caught the beach and he searched for Lucía, and for a split second, he didn't see her. His stomach began to freefall until he spotted her sitting with his mother and John, his niece and nephew playing in the sand nearby.

His chest felt tight as he looked at her beaming at him, her smile brighter than the sun. She was so beautiful she took his breath away. Her injuries had healed, the doctor had signed her off just this morning. More than that, she looked happy. Her complexion clear, she smiled all the time and charmed literally everyone she met.

His family adored her, and she fit in as if she'd been made for them, helping his mother in the garden and shopping with Caleb and even discussing architecture with John. But it was the way she played with the kids, unafraid to get dirty and be silly, which showed who she really was.

As he walked toward her, taking in the olive skin of her long shapely legs in the red one-piece she wore, he felt his stomach tighten with desire. Never in all his life had he met a more sensual woman. Lucía held nothing of herself back when she was with him, giving him everything. Her response to his touch lit a fire in his veins making him wonder how he'd possibly be able to walk away from her at the end of their time in Cairns.

Sunglasses covered most of her face as she glanced up at him with a smile, the floppy hat she'd bought protecting her from the brutality of the Australian sun. She was sitting with her knees pulled up, her arms hugging them loosely and it made him want to bend down and take her sweet mouth in a kiss that would curl her toes, but with his family watching he kept his need in check.

"You were great. I didn't know you surfed."

He flopped down next to her, shaking his head, the water droplets landing on her skin and she laughed batting her hand at him.

"Hey, you got me wet."

A smirk twitched on his face and he leaned in closer so only she could hear his words. "You get me hard so we're even."

The little hitch in her breath had him rolling on his front to conceal the fact he was now hard for her. His dick ached to be inside her, to feel her warm heat squeezing him as she found her release.

"Justice, your mum is right there."

Her prim manner sometimes made him grin, especially as he knew how wild and uninhibited she was in the bedroom. "She can't hear, and what do you expect with you looking like a fucking vision? I swear to God, Lucía, you're the most stunning woman I've ever laid eyes on, and the things I want to do to you are probably illegal in about half the world."

A groan left her lips, and he felt the answering animalistic growl reverberate in his throat. Watching her squirm, her legs shifting as if to ease the ache he knew he'd caused, he felt caught in his own trap.

"Hey, love birds, we're going to get ice cream. Do you want

anything?" Caleb stood over them, his shades covering his eyes, his son Jake hopping from foot to foot in excitement.

"No, thank you, Caleb, but some water when you come back would be nice."

"Water. Got it, Princess, and for you, my lord?"

Reaper and Lucía hadn't hidden what they were doing from his family, and he'd explained to them it was a fling, a temporary bit of fun like all his past associations. Yet even as he'd said it, the words had felt bitter in his mouth like a betrayal to Lucía in some way. "Just water, minion."

Caleb rolled his eyes. "I despair of you sometimes, Justice."

Reaper watched his brother walk away before his gaze came back to Lucía. She was looking out to sea, a beatific look on her face, and he wondered again how he was going to walk away from her when this was over. The last weeks had taught him that there was so much more to her than the photographer or the Princess. Both lived inside her, but she was so much more.

"Have you heard from Bás today?"

Her question surprised him. She'd seemed content to let him handle that side of it, not asking about the investigation and he'd been glad, because the truth was, it was slow. Glancing around he didn't see Bishop or Hurricane, nor Valentina and her furry friends, but he knew they were close and watching his back.

"Not today, but he normally calls at night because of the time difference unless it's urgent."

Her face angled toward him, and he sat, his erection gone now the conversation had turned to work and her safety. Sitting with his knees pulled up, elbows resting on them, he watched a boat far out to sea as a jet ski sped along the coastline.

"Is there an update?"

He wasn't sure what had prompted her to ask, and his stomach tensed in a way he didn't like as if expecting a blow. "From the text messages we found on Felix's phone we believe he was being blackmailed into divulging information on you, and he was the one that leaked your alias." He didn't tell her it was because of the proof they'd found of his obsession and love for the King or that his entire apartment had been like a shrine to King Juan. Yet, as far as they could tell, his involvement had seemed unwilling. What they didn't know was how the blackmailers found out he'd been about to tell Lucía of his involvement and throw himself on his sword.

"Do you know who was blackmailing him?"

"No, but we have a link to a man from my past. When it originally came up, I thought perhaps the threat was made because of me but it wasn't."

Her head swung to him, her face shocked, her skin pale despite the sun. "What? Who?"

He couldn't take her looking at him like that and not touch her, so he reached a hand out to stroke the skin on her cheek, his protective instincts kicking in when she leaned into his palm like a kitten seeking shelter and warmth. "A man named Parker Richardson, but I knew him as Playboy. He was on my team when I was in the military. He committed a heinous crime when we were deployed. I caught him and I lost it. I beat him until we had to carry him out."

"What happened?" As if sensing this didn't end as it should she leaned in close, offering him comfort as he took a walk down memory lane that he most definitely didn't want to take but with her, it was somehow easier.

"I reported him thinking he'd be disciplined but the only person to have any come back was me. Even though my some of teammates backed me, the ones that didn't seemed to sway the top brass by saying they hadn't seen what I had, and Parker's father was a powerful man. I got a dishonourable discharge for my trouble. I've hated him since and the feeling is mutual."

"I'm so sorry. You did a good thing, an honourable thing, and you got punished instead of commended."

Reaper shrugged as she leaned on his arm, kissing his shoulder. "It's fine. I came to terms with it and found my place with Shadow.

They're a true team. They'd die for me, and I'd lay down my life for them."

"They're good people."

He nodded slowly. "They are. Not in the conventional sense that society dictates but yes, they're good people."

"So, you think this man is targeting me, but why?"

He shook his head, none of the searches had come back with any leads. "I don't know but you're a threat to him in some way." His head dipped to hers and he kissed her hair, loving the scent of the sea and her shampoo when his lips touched her head.

"Have you any idea?"

Lucía shook her head. "No, I figured I was a target for who I was, not what I had seen but there is one thing. A photograph I took a long time ago, but I don't have a way to identify the man in the image and nobody would print it."

Reaper sat straighter, his gut telling him this was important, and he angled toward her, gently grasping her biceps. "Where is it?"

"On a thumb drive. I keep it on my key ring."

He shook his head at the naivete of doing such a thing, then wondered if she wasn't right to keep it close. "Do you have it with you?"

"It's back at the house. Why? Do you think it might be important?"

"I don't know but I think it's worth us taking a look. We can have Watchdog go through and see if it's linked in some way."

Lucía jumped to her feet and began packing up her stuff, looking down at him as she paused. "Come on, we need to go."

He stood and helped her pack up and shot a text to Bishop that they might have something and to wait for his instructions. The reply was instant.

"I thought someone lit a fire under your girl."

"She ain't my girl."

"You sure about that? Because if Bás saw what I did, he'd have your balls in a vice."

"It's not his business or yours, so butt out."

"Roger that, pretty boy."

Caleb had luckily brought his own car, so Reaper shot him a quick text to let him know they were headed home. His hand on Lucía's back, his body alert for any danger, he walked to the car. Suddenly it felt like the outside world was crashing back in and he knew why he'd put off this conversation with her until she brought it up. It was because he didn't want to find a reason to cut what they had short.

CHAPTER 16

Lucía felt a sense of urgency in the pit of her stomach that mixed with a sudden feeling of dread. The minute she'd mentioned the photograph that had shaped her career, the reality of her life had become real again, this vacation from the real world ending abruptly. Rushing towards the bag where she kept her keys for the cottage, she rooted around inside and grasped the bundle. Justice stood at her back, his large body covering hers, the awareness from earlier still thrumming through her blood, and he touched her shoulder as if grounding her.

She dragged the keys out and shoved them at him as he frowned at the fluffy teddy keyring. "Here."

"What's this?"

His confusion would've been comical if not for the seriousness of the situation. Lucía took the keys from him and began to unscrew the teddy bear's head to reveal a USB drive.

His eyebrows rose and he took it back. "Ingenious."

She smiled at his back as he headed for the door. She followed as he went to his room and logged into his computer, which had been secured by Watchdog so it was safe to use.

His fingers were swift over the keys, and she wondered if there was anything this man couldn't do. Her body heated with the memories of what those hands had done to her and how much pleasure he'd given her.

"Password?"

Lucía had at least password protected the drive, knowing she wouldn't want just anyone seeing the images which were so disturbing. "Fuck it."

Reaper looked at her, his face a mask and not showing his emotions, but the ticking in his jaw gave him away. "Not really a helpful attitude right now, Princess."

"No, the password is Fuckit. One word, capital F."

He smirked. "Nice."

"I can never remember my passwords, so I always end up saying *Fuckit.*"

Reaper shook his head, but he was smiling as he typed it in, and the file opened. Lucía pointed to the folder, and he clicked on it. The image hit her screen, and like it had at the time, and every time since that night, her breath left her body in a deluge of grief and pain.

The air stilled around her, and it took her a second to realise that Justice had gone stone still beside her, his body like marble, not a single muscle moving as if even the breath in his body had turned to stone.

"Justice?" He turned to her then and she dragged her eyes away from the painful image on the screen. "Do you know him, Justice?"

Her hands moved to his shoulders, and he stood, moving away from her as if her touch burned. She tried to push away the feeling of hurt and give him the space he needed as he faced the window, the bright Australian sun not reflecting the sudden dark mood in the room.

"I told you about the man in my team I caught committing a crime."

Her lungs seized as if the air didn't know whether to leave or suffocate her and she reached out to grab the bed for support. An intense feeling of dread worked its way up her spine. "Yes."

"That's the image I saw. I walked around the corner after patrolling the other side of the village and saw him raping that girl and lost my mind. I beat him half to death until my other team members pulled me off him. I would've killed him, wanted to kill him for what he'd done."

He turned to face her then and she could see the torment in his eyes. The devastation and guilt were like a shroud pulling at him. Tears filled her eyes as the pain and fury she saw in him hit her like a bullet. The realisation that they'd shared the same horrific experience was hard to swallow. In some way, it made sense to her. More and more she was starting to think Justice was meant to be in her life, and this was like a confirmation of that.

Reaching for him seemed natural and his arms came around her, holding her close, her body touching his from chest to toe. He cradled her head in his hand and she felt a kiss on her head as she snuggled closer to his body and the security and comfort he offered.

She felt a shiver go through him. "I can't stand the thought of you witnessing that. Of being so close to that evil, of seeing what I did."

Lucía pulled her head back so she could look at him, but his arms stayed closed around her waist, keeping her near him. "I didn't see you attack him. In fact, I didn't see you at all." Shame at what she'd done flooded her once more, and the guilt she carried tightened around her chest. Dropping her head, she sucked in a breath as tears hit her eyes.

"Hey, talk to me."

Reaper led her to the bed and sat her down, before crawling on the bed beside her and tucking her into his body.

"I ran, Justice. I saw what he was doing, and panic seized me like a vice. I could hardly breathe at the horror I was seeing. To this day I don't know why I took that photo. It was like instinct and then I heard a noise. Instead of stepping in to stop what was happening, I ran. Oh, God, I left her to her fate. She was a child and I was such a coward."

"No, you did the right thing. Playboy and Chess could have hurt you. You had no idea if help was close, or if they would've done the same thing to you."

"But she was only sixteen years old."

"I know." He kissed her nose and her eyelids, and she leaned into his touch. Tilting her head up she caught his lips with her own. The kiss started as comfort but quickly turned heated as she sat up, straddling his thighs.

Justice looked up at her, his hand sweeping out to cup her neck so he could pull her into his kiss. She might be the one instigating this but there was no doubt who was in control as he swept her away with a kiss so dominant and demanding she could do nothing but give herself over to him.

Feelings of guilt and shame were pushed away with the power of the desire they shared. He never made her feel like she was untouchable like a China doll. He made her feel precious and desirable in a way nobody ever had before.

Lucía's hands feathered over the material of his tee, feeling the warm skin as she pushed the fabric up and away. Justice broke the kiss for a moment to haul the shirt away before his lips were back on her skin. Kissing her bare shoulder, his fingers flicked the straps of the swimsuit down to reveal her breasts, aching and heavy with the need to be touched.

Lifting his head, the flame of passion was evident in his dark eyes as all her defences, even the ones she hadn't realised she was holding on to, came crashing down.

"Fucking perfection."

His growl before his thumb rubbed over a pert nipple made her whimper with want. Goosebumps broke out on her skin as he plucked at her nipple, his mouth finding hers again as their tongues duelled, seeking more.

Need chased her as Justice kissed his way down her neck, the stubble on his face abrading her skin and making the need coil tighter inside her. Her breath came in short pants, her hands ran over his chest, the hair springy under her fingertips.

Justice latched onto her nipple, his hungry mouth pulling and sucking, his teeth toying with her sensitive bud as his hands gripped her hips, rocking her core against the hard ridge of his cock.

Never in her life had she felt this kind of pleasure, but it wasn't enough. She needed more from him, she needed everything. As if reading her mind, Justice flipped them so she was on her back, his hard body over hers before he kissed her again, his hands peeling the swimsuit and the wrap covering her from the sun down her body. Naked and exposed, she looked at him as he pulled back to strip his own clothes away.

His body was magnificent, all hard lines and planes of ridged muscle and sinew. His cock jutted proudly from his body and drew her eyes down. She reached for him, aching to touch the skin she knew would be hot and silky.

Justice chuckled, backing up a step. "Hold on there, angel. If you touch me now, this will be over."

Lucía pouted and his warm laugh swept through her, adding an even more intimate layer to their closeness. Her gaze was pulled toward him as he bent to get a condom. He gripped his cock in his strong hand and stroked twice from root to tip, in a maddening tease. A low moan slipped from her throat and he watched her, his eyes moving over her slowly as if taking in every inch of her exposed frame and seeing into her soul.

"Stop teasing and get yourself over here."

Light danced in his eyes as he bent toward her, nestling between her legs, the tip of his cock brushing against her opening. His mouth caught hers as he rested his elbows on either side of her head, caging her in so all she could see and feel and smell was him, consuming her in the best way.

Lucía arched her back trying to get closer to him, her body aching to have the empty feeling inside her filled. Running her hands along his chest, she used her nails and felt him shudder against her skin as he broke the kiss and looked down at her before reaching for her hands. Linking their fingers, he held them above her head and thrust into her, hard and fast.

The intrusion of his body made her gasp in pleasure and pain. Justice waited a beat, his eyes on her again watching, waiting for her to say she was okay, and she nodded.

"Move. Please, Justice."

His jaw flexing with the control to stay still, he let out a breath and began to move. Using his body, his hands, and his mouth to drive her to the pinnacle of pleasure time and again until she was boneless, begging for release. He knew her body so well, knew every single place on her skin that made her whimper.

His teeth toyed with her nipple, his pelvic bone rocking against her clit on each thrust until she teetered on the edge of climax. One final thrust and she was hurtling down, her body splintering apart with such intense feelings of pleasure she couldn't hold back the sob that tore from her.

"That's it, angel, let go. Fuck you're so beautiful and you're mine. Nobody gets to see this but me."

Lucía could hardly comprehend the words let alone reply, but Justice was relentless, pushing her again and again until she thought she'd die from too much blood leaving her brain.

"Who do you belong to, Lucía?"

His voice was a growl and demanded that she answer, and she knew in her heart exactly who she belonged to. She was just terrified that she'd never get to feel the same. "You, Justice. I belong to you."

"Fucking right you do, and I belong to you."

Out of nowhere, his words hit her and she felt her body respond. The impending climax tightened her body and this time he fell with her, his release filling her as his groan of ecstasy filled the air. His body flopped down onto hers as she embraced him, holding him close and wishing the words they said were real and they could find a way to make this work. But her life didn't work that way. It had never been her own, and she was a fool to think it would be any different this time.

Cherishing the feeling and embracing the moment, she held tighter until he got up to go and deal with the condom. Curling on her side, she knew she was in love with Justice. She had no idea how she'd survive losing him, but that was a problem for another day. She'd promised herself and him this time, and she'd enjoy every second of it and worry about the rest when she was on her own with nothing but time.

CHAPTER 17

"Line's secure. Reaper, go ahead."

Sitting in his room with Lucía beside him as they faced his team on the screen, it was hard to keep his hands to himself or his thoughts from what they'd shared not an hour ago. Her hair was wet from the shower they'd taken, her skin flushed from the sun and what they'd shared.

Shaking his head slightly he tried to concentrate on his team-mates so he could do the job he was here to do, and that was to keep her safe. "We think we've found what Playboy and his men are looking for. It's a picture Lucía took of him attacking a girl when we were on that last mission."

Bishop, who was patched in from the safe house, frowned. "Wait, you never mentioned you knew Lucía before this op."

Justice glanced at her, and even in his own mind, it was hard to consider how this could've happened. "No, we never met."

"I wasn't meant to be in the village, but our vehicle had broken down not far from there. The elder said we could stay the night until we could get it fixed. I was wandering the village taking pictures when I heard a noise and saw what I did."

"Jesus, do you know how close you came to being exposed?"

Bás' harsh tone had Justice's hackles going up in her defence. "Of course she does, so don't fucking start, Bás."

A pair of intelligent, seeing eyes met his through the camera and he knew his boss was watching him for tells, which he studiously tried not to give.

"Enough with the drama, the why doesn't matter right now. What matters is how he figured out about the picture and your identity." Duchess cut through the bullshit with her words, her demeanour not broking any argument.

"Did you try and sell the picture to any of the nationals, Princess Lucía?"

Lucía shook her head, her fingers playing with the edge of her skirt, belying her nerves. "No, I tried to sell it to Geographic for a piece on the cost of war but decided I didn't want it out in the world and the girl's humiliation to be fodder for the masses. I did ask around about the soldier though but got nowhere."

"Then that's where we start." Bás had taken Duchess' lead but Reaper had no doubt that he'd hear about this again, his boss didn't give up. "Watchdog, dig into everyone at Geographic and see if any tie back to either Reaper, Playboy, or the Princess in any way. Bishop, talk to your contacts and find out if there was any push back from Princess Lucía's enquiries into the operation when this happened."

Bishop groaned. "Ah, come on, boss. You know the only contact I have there is an evil shrew with the integrity of rice paper."

"Listen, I get it, but we need something, and she's the best bet for this."

"Fine, but if I end up in a morgue in some God-forsaken country then it's on you."

Bás rolled his eyes. "She won't kill you."

Bishop looked affronted. "May I remind you she shot me and left me for dead?"

"I don't blame her. If I'd been married to you, I might do the same."

Bishop threw up his hands. "Fine, whatever, I'll reach out to her."

"Good, now we have another matter to discuss and that's the hack on our system."

Reaper saw Watchdog clench his teeth and worried his canines would crumble from the force.

"Watchdog shut it down but we know they were looking at the file we have on the Princess."

Reaper sat up straighter, his senses firing up and suddenly the reality of it all slammed back into him. He was meant to be protecting her not having a fucking family holiday. "We need to move her."

Bás held up his hand. "Hold your horses, we think she's safe there for now."

"Have we found Playboy or Chess yet?"

Bás sighed and that one action spoke a thousand words about how his boss and friend was feeling. "No, those fuckers are slipperier than an eel covered in baby oil. Last known location was three months ago in New York and yes, before you ask, I've already sent Rykov to speak to the people he was meeting."

Reaper bristled at being kept out of the loop on important information. "Why didn't you tell me before?"

"Because until this morning it was an unconfirmed sighting and I can't be sending my team on a wild goose chase."

Reaper didn't like it, but he understood Bás was juggling a lot.

"Playboy met with a man called Yakiv Petrovych Fedorchuk. He's a Romanian Diplomat in the United States and has a very murky background. He's ex-military and served in the Romanian armed forces. Had a few years where we have nothing on him and then he pops up in this job. Watchdog is still looking into him but what we do know is that he's not good news. Playboy meeting him can only mean bad news."

Reaper brushed his hands through his hair. "Rykov makes sense."

"Exactly and he can use his own men as cover for this."

"Fine, let me know what Rykov finds out."

"Until then, Snow is watching the Richardson family with Titan. He might go home at some point so it's worth a punt."

"He was a daddy's boy so, yeah, perhaps."

Bás nodded. "Now we can try and use the hacker, but they're in Germany, so we're sending Lotus, and Bein, to find him or her and question them. If that yields nothing, we may need to be more obvious."

Reaper sat up straighter, he had a feeling he wouldn't like this. "Meaning?"

"We bring the Princess back to the Palace."

"No fucking way. She's way too exposed there. Anything could happen to her, and we can't trust the guard."

"King Juan fired his head of security two days ago, and thanks to a report we gave him on the others, he's cleaning house as we speak. She'll be safe. Eidolon have also offered to help."

Eidolon was their parent team and the more well-known, but no less deadly or qualified at protection, having been protecting the Queen for near on six years. Reaper knew it made sense to draw Playboy and his team out and end this for good, but he wasn't willing to take the chance. Not with her, not with Lucía. "No, I won't have her put in danger."

"Do I get a say in this?"

Reaper glanced at the woman he was breaking all his rules for and shook his head. "No, not with this, Lucía. I can't risk you getting hurt." He prayed she understood he was coming from a good place and didn't fight him. Yes, he was making a unilateral decision about her safety, but he needed her to trust him when it came to her safety more than he could say.

"Fine but if things change, we do it his way. I can't spend my life being hunted, Justice."

Reaper gritted his teeth and nodded, knowing he had no other choice. Seeing the haunted look in her eyes over the last few hours as the memory of the video returned had been agony, and he knew how much it was affecting her.

Bás grinned but it was anything but warm and friendly, and Reaper knew he'd been caught with his own net. "I see. Well, let's try the hacker first and see if Bishop can find any information."

Not particularly wanting to have the conversation but knowing it might be a good source of information, Reaper made the offer anyway. "I can speak to my father and see if he knows anything."

Duchess angled her head, her dark hair falling across her neck and the myriad of tattoos adorning the slender column, visible. "You sure about this, Reaper?"

"Yeah, it makes sense. He still has contacts in the military."

"Okay, if you're sure."

Reaper glanced at Lucía who was watching him, clearly over-whelmed by it all and suffocating in ghosts from the past. "I am."

"Which brings us to the next question, Princess Lucía's visit to the Middle East. I know we said we'd do everything we could to make this happen, but given the number of unknowns in the mix, I don't conceivably see how it can happen safely at this time."

Reaper felt a sliver of relief go through him that Bás had brought this up. Since the image had come through and he'd realised how much danger she was in, he'd been dreading pulling the rug from under her and saying she had to cancel. Especially as he now knew the purpose of the trip was to check on the girl from the photograph. The one he knew was already dead.

The air from the AC cooled his heated skin but did nothing to ease the sadness in his heart as he accepted he had to tell her and knowing it would break her heart. He desperately wanted to reach for her, hating that they had to hide this from his boss as if what they shared was dirty instead of the beauty he'd found with her.

He hadn't lied when he'd said she was his. Making love to her had cemented something inside of him. The thought of her being with anyone else sent a sharp splinter through his gut. He just didn't know if he deserved a woman like her. No, scratch that. He knew he wasn't good enough and yet he wanted her anyway. He just wasn't sure he could find a way to make it happen or if it was even what Lucía wanted.

Perhaps he was her bit of rough before she settled down with a Duke or Prince, someone more suited to her standing in life. A man who could stand beside her proudly, not one who was, in essence, a glorified killer. What he did know was that whatever man she ended up with, he'd need to be extraordinary to be good enough for her.

"Reaper?"

He shook himself from the thoughts overriding his brain and glanced at Lucía. "Sorry, what?"

"I asked if you agreed with Bás?"

He nodded and reached for her hand off-camera, feeling her silky skin warm against his rough, calloused hand. "Yes, I agree with Bás. Maybe when this is all handled you can rearrange the visit but currently, it's too dangerous. There are too many variables to deal with and it would end up with someone getting hurt or worse."

"I see." Her head dropped before she seemed to rally, straightening her spine, and lifting her head in such a regal manner it was hard for him to understand how the whole world didn't see the amazing woman he did, despite the disguises she wore for her job. "Well, given that, I'll cancel or rather postpone the visit and reschedule when things are more settled, but I want to go." Her eyes came to him then, imploring him to understand. "I need to know what happened to her."

Reaper squeezed her hand, hating that he had to tell her and break her heart. "I understand and we'll figure something out."

Lucía nodded once. "Okay, well if that's all you need from me, I might go and visit with Caleb and John while you talk about whatever it is secret special ops people talk about."

His family had just arrived back from the beach and the timing was perfect. Reaper watched her leave, his eyes moving over her as he tried his best to hide his increasing feelings for her.

The door closed firmly behind her, he turned back to the screen to see, Bás and Duchess were the only two still on the call.

"What the fuck, Reaper?"

He could deny it and pretend he didn't know what his boss was talking about, but this team only worked because of the transparency and honesty among them all. No matter how painful this conversation was going to be, he needed to have it. "I care about her, Bás."

"I don't give a flying fuck. You knew the rules and you broke them. What the fuck is happening to you all? Falling in love every two fucking seconds."

"It's not love, I just..." He stopped because how could he quantify how he felt about her when every thought or sentence made it sound more and more like love. But that wasn't the plan, he didn't put down roots. He was too much like his father, too selfish to love anyone and commit to their happiness over his own, wasn't he? "I didn't plan this."

"Reaper, you may not see this but it's clear as day from where I'm sitting that Princess Lucía is in love with you and if I'm not very much mistaken, the feeling is mutual. If it isn't, you need to end it right now."

Reaper looked at Duchess as she spoke her words softer than Bás but her warning as stark. "I will."

The words felt like a betrayal, his gut twisting painfully at the thought of ending things, but he knew they were right. If he didn't love her as she deserved, he had no business dragging this out no matter how much he wanted to. To think he'd been trying to come up with ways to keep this going between them and not giving thought to how much he could hurt the beautiful, strong, tenacious, and kind woman made him feel ashamed.

"Good and you need to tell her about the girl. She needs to know she's dead."

"I know."

"Do you want me to tell her? It might be easier and more clinical if it came from me."

Reaper appreciated Bás' offer but this was his mess. "No, I'll tell her."

Bás gave a short nod. "Do you need me to have Bishop take over?"

"No, I can handle this." The thought of anyone else watching over Lucía just didn't sit right with him.

"Good, stay safe and I'd say behave but that horse has well and truly bolted. Just don't be a dick."

"Fuck you, Bás. Duchess, always a pleasure." Reaper hit end on the call not wanting to waste any more time on this when he wanted to be with Lucía. The feeling of time running out was like a runaway train and it was headed right for him.

CHAPTER 18

"Will you stop looking in the fucking mirror. The Princess will be fine with Hurricane and Valentina. Especially with those mutts of hers standing guard."

Reaper held on to the handle above his head as Bishop took a turn too fast, his glare sliding off the man like he was coated in Teflon. "I'm not worried."

Bishop smirked as he stopped at a traffic light. "You know, I never thought you'd be next. I had my money on Hurricane."

That got his attention and he turned toward Bishop as the light turned green. "What makes you say that?"

Bishop shook his head like he was an imbecile. "Are you sure you're smart?"

"I'll throw you out of this moving car, Bishop, if you keep annoying me."

"Fine, he was making googly eyes at that friend of Aoife's."

Reaper frowned. "You mean Payton?"

"Yeah, poor bloke is gone for her, but she doesn't seem interested."

"Huh, I didn't see that coming."

"No shit. Well, we didn't see you falling in love with a Princess either."

"We aren't in love."

Bishop smirked again as they pulled into the neighbourhood where his father lived. "You keep telling yourself that. You were like a mother fucking hen before we left."

"Are you surprised? Playboy is a nasty piece of work and if he gets his hands on her...." He couldn't finish that thought and keep his cool, and as he was about to meet with his father for the first time in five years he needed to.

"Man, I get it. When Storm and I were together I was the same."

Bishop never really spoke about his ex-wife except to call her duplicitous and evil but Reaper wasn't a fool and Bishop wasn't the actor he thought he was because he could hear the hurt in his voice every time he spoke of her.

Reaper pointed at the house. "Pull up here."

Bishop pulled over to the side of the road. The house was small but immaculate, the lawn looked like it had been cut with nail scissors. The shutters were clean and the glass didn't have a speck of dust.

Reaper knew his father had retired shortly after his parents' marriage broke down, but he was still a military man at heart and obviously kept the same standards as he always had.

As he and Bishop got out of the car, the front door opened, and Reaper felt like he'd been thrown back in time. The feelings of not being good enough, of not being strong enough barrelled down on him as if that little boy seeking approval was still inside him buried deep. He wasn't that child any longer though. He was a man, and he was here to protect the woman he now knew owned his heart.

"Son, this is a surprise."

On closer inspection, his father looked older, weaker somehow, not as invincible as he'd seemed growing up. He was still dressed in a formal shirt and tie, a crease down the front of his trousers as if he expected someone of importance to turn up.

"Dad, I hope you don't mind me dropping by like this."

The fact was, Reaper had discussed it with Val, Hurricane, and Bishop and catching his father off guard had seemed the best approach. He didn't trust him and giving him more time seemed counterproductive.

"Of course not. Come in."

Reaper stepped inside with Bishop following his lead. The home was sparse with as little furniture as possible. Two easy chairs, a television, and a coffee table. The kitchenette had a small table with four chairs. There weren't any pictures on the walls or clutter of any kind, and Reaper wondered how his father could go from living in such warmth as their family home to this cold nothingness.

"This is my friend Bishop."

"Nice to meet you, Bishop. Any friend of my son is welcome here."

Reaper didn't know where the friendly behaviour was coming from, but he didn't trust it. His father always liked to come across as nice but when it was just the two of them, he was a bastard.

"Would you like some water, tea, coffee?"

"Water would be good, thanks."

Reaper followed his father into the kitchen that led to a small, terraced area. His gait was off. The usual upright, almost military march his father had was gone and had been replaced by an irregular gait and he'd lost weight too.

His father handed him and Bishop a glass of ice-cold water and indicated they sit at the bare kitchen table. Reaper sat opposite his dad, the man who'd made him who he was in some ways and felt a flicker of sadness for the man in front of him who had nobody in his life that seemed to care or mean anything to him.

"Mr Carson, Reaper and I would like to ask you a few questions if that's possible."

His father curled his lip. "Reaper?"

"I apologise. Justice."

His father's eyes, so like his own, came to his, and yet they held none of the warmth he hoped he had. "Is that what they call you?"

Reaper locked his jaw. "Yes."

Malcolm Carson glanced at Bishop, his eyes assessing now. "You work with my son at the search and rescue place?"

"Yes, sir, I do."

Malcolm shook his head, his hand shaking slightly as he lifted the water to his lips. "Damn waste of a fine soldier."

"I wouldn't agree with that, Mr Carson."

"Colonel Carson," his father corrected.

Bishop shot him a look but spared the eye roll he knew he wanted to give him at his father's ridiculous posturing.

"Enough, Dad. Can we ask you a few questions or not?"

An impatient sigh rolled through his chest and Malcolm waved his hand. "Get on with it then."

Reaper sat forward a little but not enough to tip his hand to how important this was. "Do you remember Parker Richardson and Micah Rawlings?"

As if a button had been pushed, he saw his father's defences go up. "Maybe, I can't remember every soldier."

"This is important, Dad, think. Parker and Rawlings went by Playboy and Chess. Do you remember? They were on my team with me."

"Yes, I remember them."

Defeat sounded in his father's voice that he'd never heard before. It made Reaper proceed with caution. "Do you remember why they left the service? Their records are sealed or non-existent and I need to know."

"Why?"

Reaper shook his head. "I can't tell you that."

Malcolm angled his head to the side. "You don't work for a search and rescue company do you, son?"

Reaper glanced at Bishop, not sure what to tell his old man. They'd locked horns more than he could say and there was no love lost between them, but Malcolm could read him better than most. "Yes and no."

His father slapped his thigh and laughed, causing him to break into a coughing fit. Reaper handed his father the water glass, cupping his hand around the glass to stabilise it as his father shook from the racking breaths shuddering through his body.

As his father got himself under control worry tinged the back of Reaper's neck. His unsteady gait, the coughing, the weight loss, it was easy to make the connection that his father was a very sick man. Reaper pulled away, dropping his hand, and pushing the sympathy he was feeling aside. This man had ruined his life and the way he'd treated Caleb and his mother was downright callous. Still, a tiny flame of regret flickered that they'd never worked out their differences.

"I knew you had more about you than that. I didn't raise a quitter and while I don't condone what you did to get kicked out of the army, it seems you found yourself a new life."

"I don't want to talk about that. I just need to know why Playboy got kicked out and if anyone has seen him lately."

Malcolm gave a short nod of understanding, his breaths finally calming into a regular rhythm since the coughing fit. "I haven't seen him since before I retired. I don't know the full story, only what I heard from friends still in the service. Shortly after I left there was a mission in Iran. I don't know the details but apparently Playboy, and that other one, Chess, were caught trying to smuggle young women across the border."

Reaper looked to Bishop, his body tensing as memories of what happened in the Hindu Kush flooded his mind. "That bastard."

Malcolm nodded his agreement. "Nothing was ever levelled against him charge wise. Most likely because of who his father is, but after what happened with you, the powers that be couldn't look the other way again."

Reaper pushed back his chair, the sound of wood scraping the floor loud in the small room. "What the hell does that mean?"

Malcolm held up a hand as if to calm his oldest son, but it was no use. Rage was bubbling up inside him, like poison lava. "Son, calm down."

"Don't tell me to calm the fuck down. You don't even know me, or who I am."

"Reaper."

He glanced at Bishop, who was still seated, a warning in his tone that he wanted to heed but anger about what had been done to him was flowing now. "Have you any idea why I was kicked out of the armed forces? The real reason, not the bullshit one they spouted about me beating up a colleague because I was out of control."

"Yes, I was on the committee that decided your fate. I heard the testimony given by the rest of your team."

Reaper reared back as if someone had sucker-punched him in the chest. "What? You were what?" Hurt tinged his words but mostly it was anger at the betrayal that was so much deeper than he'd thought.

"Sit down please and let me explain."

"No, fuck this. I'm done with you."

Reaper brushed past Bishop and went outside to wait for his friend, sucking in oxygen to calm the tirade of rage inside him. How could he still have this noose around his neck from trying to do the right thing? Even his own father had betrayed him, cutting him loose and never saying a single word about it.

"Reaper."

Turning, he saw Bishop striding toward him, his cocky swagger an act, just as much as the overly London accent he put on. "You ready to go?"

"Reaper, you should hear him out."

"No, he gave up that right when he sold me out."

"How do you know he sold you out? You never even stopped to listen."

"Because I know the man he is, and family doesn't come first for my father."

"Maybe, but it seems to me that you won't always have the luxury of getting to ask him. He's clearly a sick man and if you don't get answers now, you may never get them. Believe me when I say you *do not* want to go the rest of your life with unanswered questions."

Everything inside him baulked at the request but something in Bishop's expression made him nod. "Fine."

"I'll wait here."

Reaper dipped his chin in acknowledgement and headed back inside to find his father standing at the sink looking out into the backyard. "Talk, old man."

"Can we sit?"

Reaper nodded, shoving his hands in his pockets to stop from reaching out to steady the weakened man as he headed into the living room and sat in a chair facing the window. Reaper took the other and waited, his hands clasped in front of him.

"We all knew Playboy and Chess were guilty. It wasn't the first complaint that had been made about them. Neither were fit to wear the uniform and we all knew it. We were all set to have them arrested on charges but at the last minute, a message came through from General Sykes that Richardson and Rawlings were to be released and no charges laid against them. I was asked to leave the room and when the others came out, your fate was sealed."

"So General Sykes is behind this?"

"No, but he's friends with Richardson Senior and is Parker Richardson's Godfather. I tried to argue against it, but nobody would listen to me. I was only a Major at that point."

Confusion gripped Reaper as he tried to tell if his father was lying to save his own skin. But whatever else he'd been and done, he'd never lied to his sons, even when he'd sometimes wished he had to save their feelings. "That's why it took you so long to make Colonel, isn't it? Because you made waves."

"Maybe. But it doesn't matter now."

Reaper swallowed back the regret he felt that they'd never had this frank openness between them before. "Are you dying, Dad?"

"Perhaps. They don't know how long I have but I'll keep fighting."

"Cancer?"

"Lung, but it spread to my bones."

"Why didn't you tell anyone?"

Malcolm looked up his eyes clear. "After the way I treated you all, why would you care? I was an awful husband and a terrible father. You're all better off without me."

"You *were* a bit of a dick."

Malcolm froze, his face stern before he laughed, making him cough again and reach for a hankie in his pocket. "I *was* a dick, and it's my biggest regret. I hate how I treated you and Caleb and your mother. She never deserved it. God, she deserved so much better than me and I have no idea why she put up with me for as long as she did. Still, it's done. No use crying about it now. I got what I deserved."

"There still might be time to make amends."

Malcolm shook his head. "No, I won't guilt them into forgiving me because they feel sorry for me, and I'm asking you not tell them, please."

Reaper shook his head, knowing he wouldn't promise that. "I can't promise that, old man. I'm my own man these days and I decide what and who and when."

His father nodded once. "Yes, you are and you're ten times the man I am. I'm proud of you, son. I know I haven't the right to say that after everything I put you through and God knows it's not because of me, but nonetheless, I'm proud of you."

Reaper coughed to cover the choked up feeling in his chest. All his life he'd wanted those words but hearing them now, he realised he didn't need them. He had the respect of far greater men than his father but he knew the man needed closure and so he gave it to him. "I don't know, you can take credit for my right hook and tenacity perhaps."

His peace offering meant a lot to the older man and as he walked out of his father's house possibly for the first and last time, he felt a sense of peace inside him he hadn't expected.

He knew the truth about what had happened the day his career had ended, and they had another thread to pull to find Playboy and Chess. That he'd been so right about them filled him with no satisfaction, just deep sadness that so many young women had most likely suffered horrid atrocities and possibly died at their hands. If he could go back in time, he wasn't sure he would've stopped with just a beating. Men like Playboy and Chess didn't deserve to breathe precious oxygen and if it was the last thing he did, he'd see them in the ground.

Reaching the car, he got inside, the cool air a relief from the sickness in his father's home.

"You good?"

"Yeah, I am actually." He proceeded to tell Bishop everything he knew from his father including his own sordid past.

Bishop curled his lip in the same disgust he felt. "Those two need to be gone."

"Oh, I'm going to make sure of it and I'm going to make sure they feel every second of it too. Now, enough about them. Let's get back to Lucía."

"Whipped, man. Whipped."

Reaper laughed but didn't deny it because the entire time he'd been away from her it had felt like a part of him was missing. He knew that it was because she'd stolen it and would never give it back.

CHAPTER 19

LUCÍA LET HER FINGERTIPS SMOOTH THROUGH THE SOFT FUR OF THE DOG lying beside her. Valentina was sitting on the other side, her hand doing the same thing. Not for the first time she wondered how Justice was getting on with his father. She knew it was hard for him, that his relationship with the man was complex and painful. Yet he'd do this for her, for her safety, and it spoke volumes toward the man he was. "How long have you known Justice?"

Val turned her head, her eyes shielded by the sun as she laid the phone she'd been texting on aside. "A few years. I started at Eidolon, the mother company to this one or at least the slightly more public company, but then I was seconded to work at Shadow to train the dogs for them and I stayed. Reaper was already there when I started."

Lucía nodded pursing her lips as the questions she wanted to ask stuck in her throat.

"Ask, Lucía."

Lucía loved how these people treated her like she was normal. The constant pressure of being in her family gave her a headache, no matter how much she loved them all. This was a nice reprive from life in the public eye. "Has Justice ever told you about his past or girl-friends or such?"

Val shook her head. "No, he's a pretty closed book. I know he hasn't been celibate, but I've never known of anyone that lasted past a night."

Jealousy, hot and painful, burned her chest as another reminder of how much she was coming to care for him. No, that was a weak word for what she felt. She'd done the unthinkable and let herself fall in love with him, even knowing it was as hopeless as it was.

"My son has never been one for relationships."

Lucía started, a blush staining her cheeks at the knowledge Elodie had caught her asking questions about Justice. She'd thought she'd gone to the shops with Caleb, John, and the kids to get steaks for grilling later. "I'm sorry, I shouldn't have asked."

Elodie reached out to take her hand between her own. "No, my sweet girl, you have every right."

"I'm going to go and get the dogs some water."

Valentina made a quick retreat and Elodie took her place beside her in the shade away from the sun. "Justice has always maintained he's too selfish for love, but I know it's my fault he's never opened his heart. Do you know he refuses to say the word goodbye? He's lost so many people he loves. Starting with his grandfather, and then my mother, and friends in the forces who never came home from combat." Elodie shook her head, grief in her eyes. "My boy has so much to give, so much heart and yet before he ever got the chance to give it, he was shown that love is pain. I should've done more to shield him."

Lucía hated the idea of this kind woman blaming herself for her son's pain. "No, he loves you and you're a wonderful mother."

"I know he loves me but that's different. Seeing you with him has shown me that Justice is open to love, and for that, I'm beyond grateful."

"Oh, I think you're mistaken. We're just having fun."

Elodie angled her head her eyes assessing. "Yes, you're having fun, but I've seen the way he looks at you and you look at him. This may have started as fun but it's more now. I pray with all my heart that you'll both fight for it, because without love, what else is there?"

Lucía stayed quiet, not sure how to respond. She couldn't deny her own feelings but she didn't want to give this kind woman, who'd opened her home and her life to her, false hope.

A low, growl came from Scout, who she realised had stayed at her side. Turning, she saw his ears pricked, his hackles high on his back in warning.

Seconds later, the doorbell rang and Elodie rose. "It's most likely the postie. I'm expecting some new bulbs I ordered off the internet."

Relaxing, Lucía stood and followed Elodie inside as she headed for the door.

Hurricane stopped her with a wide smile. "Let me, Mrs Carson."

Elodie rolled her eyes, not fully aware of the danger surrounding her or at least not taking it seriously and she was glad for that. The idea of her being frightened because she'd let Lucía stay was like bile in her mouth.

Moving through the kitchen and away from the door, she saw Hurricane answer the door and then everything was a blur as Monty and Scout began to bark. Valentina shouted a warning and pulled her towards the back exit into the garden.

The next thing she knew her body was being thrown into the air as an explosion rocked through the house. Screams and barking ricocheted through the room, the smell of smoke a now-familiar one.

Blinking as she coughed, Lucía pushed up to realise it hadn't been the explosion that knocked her over but Valentina, who was now lying on top of her. Dragging her body into a sitting position, she touched her friend's hair and heard her groan and reach for her head.

Relief, sharp and pungent, flooded Lucía as she let out a trembling breath. "Are you okay?"

Valentina nodded and began to push herself up. "We need to get you out of here."

A whistle pierced the air and Scout and Monty ran toward the sound, their noses buried in their owner's hair as she spoke quietly to them. The two dogs ran off and Val stood, reaching for Lucía.

"We need to check on Elodie and Hurricane. They were in the living room when the blast went off." A sick feeling of dread made it almost impossible to breathe.

"No, we need to get you out of here, now."

Lucía faced the woman she knew was trying to protect her and held her ground. "I won't run and leave them when they need our help."

"Damnit, Lucía, Playboy and Chess could be out there right now. We need to get you away from here."

A resolute feeling that she was facing her future in some way and that the decision she made now would affect the rest of her life. "Please, Val. I can't leave them."

"Fine but you do what I say and if I say run, you don't fucking hesitate."

Lucía nodded, ignoring the ache in her head and the ringing in her ears. As Val stepped in front of her they made their way back to the main room to see Hurricane and Elodie both unconscious on the floor. Scout and Monty sat by each of them, licking their faces as if trying to wake them up.

The room wasn't as bad as she'd expected, a curtain rail hung off the wall, a side table was broken, and the glass from the front door was smashed. Dust was everywhere and smoke now receded out of the front door, but it was enough devastation to make her shudder. A groan from Elodie made her drop to her knees, the shock of the explosion turning to adrenalin.

Taking Elodie's hand, which was bleeding from a cut where the glass had been imbedded, she stroked the woman's face lightly. Valentina was tending to Hurricane as she spoke rapid-fire into her phone. Scout was now positioned at the front door and Monty was behind her as if acting as a shield surrounding them all.

"Elodie, it's me. Can you hear me?"

Another groan sounded as Justice's mum tried to move. "What happened?"

Tears stung her eyes, but she blinked them away. She didn't need to fall apart right now, she needed to be strong. "There was an explosion."

Elodie blinked as she tried to sit up. "Where are Caleb and the kids?"

"They went out, remember? To the shops for steaks."

Lucía saw the confusion on Elodie's face, and it concerned her. Could she have a head injury?

"Lucía, Mum?"

She turned at the sound of his voice, the fear and urgency in it speaking of his feelings for them both. "Justice!"

He ran toward them as Bishop stopped to help Valentina with Hurricane, who seemed to be coming around now.

Falling to the floor, he took her in his arms and held her tight, almost too tight as he seemed to breathe her in for a second, reassuring himself she was okay. Pulling back, he began to run his hands over her body, not in a sexual way but looking for injuries, his eyes darting all over her, his jaw tense with worry. "Are you okay?"

"I'm fine. Valentina threw me out of the way. Your mum and Hurricane were the ones hurt."

He glanced at his mother then, before releasing her and gently reaching for his mother. "Mum, can you move your legs?"

"Yes, of course I can. It's just a little bump. You should go and see to your friend."

"I think she hit her head on the coffee table."

Elodie shook her head and then winced. "I'm fine, really."

"I want you checked out at the hospital. Both of you."

Lucía knew when to argue and now wasn't the time. Sirens rent the air of the quiet neighbourhood as Bishop walked towards them. Justice stood but kept a hand on her the entire time as if he couldn't bear to be too far away and she was glad for it. Right now, his presence was the only thing keeping her from falling apart.

"How is he?"

"Pissed off, but I think that's more because he feels responsible. He'll live. He's had worse in the ring with Lotus."

"Haven't we all." Justice glanced at her. "What happened?"

Police and ambulances were now appearing, and the area was swarming with first responders.

"A knock came at the door and your mum thought it was some stuff she'd ordered from the internet. She went to answer it, but Hurricane stopped her. I came into the kitchen to get some water, and Valentina was behind me. Then I heard a shout from Hurricane, and I was being thrown to the ground and the world was exploding."

Justice's jaw flexed, and she could see he was trying to get his temper and anger under control.

Bishop nodded. "That ties with what Hurricane is saying. Apparently, it was a package left on the doorstep. As he bent to pick it up, he saw it was addressed to Princess Lucía. That's when he shouted the warning. It was lucky he got those five seconds, or he certainly wouldn't be talking right now."

"We need to get Lucía out of here."

Bishop looked grim but nodded once. "Agreed. I'm going to call Bás while the paramedics looks these guys over."

"Yeah, okay."

"You think this is your father?"

Lucía watched as Justice went still. "No, I don't believe so, but we can't rule anything out."

As paramedics came toward her, Justice's phone rang, and he reluctantly stepped back so she could be checked over. Lucía kept her eyes on Justice as he spoke and saw the second the blood seemed to leave his face.

CHAPTER 20

His heart was still racing with the aftereffects of the adrenalin that had punched through him when he'd turned the corner into his childhood home and seen the smoke. His eyes strayed to Lucía again as he hit answer on his phone without looking. "Yes."

"You were always so predictable, Reaper, going home to Mummy."

Ice slid through his veins at the sound of Playboy's voice. Not out of fear but from the cold rage that settled low in his gut. "You come anywhere near Lucía or my family again, I'm going to personally slit your throat."

A husky laugh came down the line as Reaper's eyes flicked to Lucía before moving around the room, evaluating every single person he didn't know for a threat.

"Now, is that any way to speak to the man who's currently holding a knife to your father's throat?"

"You mother fucker. If you hurt him, so help me God...."

"Shut up and listen. If you want to see him alive again then you'll hand that little bitch over."

"Never."

"What's the matter, Reaper? Did you get attached to that sweet pussy of hers? I have to admit, I can't wait to see if she's a screamer. Does she scream for you, Reaper or is she silent like that little bitch in the desert was?"

His blood was pounding in his head as the fury built inside him. "You're going down, Playboy. I'm going to gut you like the pig you are."

"I'm just getting started. Now, bring her to the address I'm going to send you in twenty-four hours or I'm going to send daddy dearest back to you in tiny pieces."

"I want proof of life." Reaper hoped like hell Watchdog could trace this call.

"Check your girlfriend's email."

The line went dead, and Reaper became aware of Bishop next to him. "He has my father. He's sending proof of life to Lucía's email."

"He must have been watching us." Bishop brushed his hands through his hair in frustration. "Dammit, Reaper, I'm sorry. I must have missed something."

"Now isn't the time for blame. We've all been caught out, not just you. What did Bás say?"

"He thinks we should keep this between us for now and take Lucía back to base. Nobody knows about it and it's like Fort Knox."

"I agree but I have this situation with my father now."

"Let me call Bás back and fill Hurricane and Valentina in on the situation." Bishop walked away leaving just the two of them.

Her hand on his arm was soft. "Justice, who was on the phone?"

He was seconds from lying to her when something in her face stopped him. He'd told enough half-truths to this amazing woman, and it was time he came clean and behaved like a protector, not a lovesick fool. "Playboy. He has my father."

Her sharp inhalation of breath made him want to reach for her, but he held back, knowing if he touched her now, he'd crumble.

"Oh my God, this is all my fault."

He did reach for her then, the guilt in her delicate voice made his

146

gut clench, but he dropped his hand before he could feel her skin under his fingers. "No, Lucía, this isn't your fault. It's him and his sick, perverted evil. I do need to get into your emails though because he sent proof of life to your work email."

"Of course."

Bishop made his way back over to them. "Hurricane and Val have this situation under control and the police will go with your mum to the hospital so she can get checked. Val is also calling Caleb to meet them there."

"What did Bás say?"

"Watchdog puts the call in the UK, but it was pinged all around the world, so difficult to say for sure. He's calling the rest of the team and putting everyone on standby. We should probably move in case he comes for Lucía."

Reaper shook his head. "He won't. If he'd wanted her, he could've grabbed her here. This is a game to him. He wants me to hand her over to him. It's all part of it."

Bishop pursed his lips and dipped his head in agreement. "Let's check that email then."

He and Bishop followed Lucía to the room where he'd spent so many nights revelling in the passion they shared, the absolute perfection of what they were together. He ignored the rumpled sheets, proof they'd stayed up all night exploring every erogenous zone on each other's bodies and concentrated on the computer she was loading up.

In less than a minute he had the evidence he needed. A short video of his father, which must have been taken directly after they'd left. In it he was bound and gagged, his defiant glare on the camera, but Reaper could see the toll it was taking on his already weakened body. "They can't be far."

Reaper could smell the scent of her perfume as she moved closer as if she needed his comfort as much as he needed to give it. Damning the weak man he was, he lifted his arm so she could slide into the curve of his body. He closed his eyes for a second as the world tilted as if righting itself and he knew it was her making his universe spin correctly. She was his strength, not his weakness, and he was a fool to push her away. Yet he couldn't see a way they could be together, so he dropped a kiss to her head and gently let her go.

The confusion and hurt in her eyes sliced him like a blade to the heart but he didn't see a way out of this without her getting hurt and he hated that. She didn't deserve any of this. She was the very best of people and he'd give anything to take away the pain she was feeling.

A ping on his phone had him looking down as a text message came through. Reaper paced away, not wanting Lucía to see but knowing he had to tell her. Frustration at always being on the back foot with this situation made him lash out his fist slamming into the wall of the bedroom. "Argh."

"Justice, what is it?"

He turned to see Bishop watching him closely, his posture calm but ready and Lucía looking more afraid than ever before, and he knew he'd done that. "He's taking my father to the UK. To Whitmore to be precise. He must have grabbed him just after we left my dad's house."

He saw the colour leave her face. "Oh my God. My friends."

"That means he's only going to be a few hours ahead of us. We need to get the team to Whitmore, now. We can leave Lucía at the base or with Eidolon."

Reaper knew Bishop was right, but he also knew how stubborn the woman glaring at them both was.

"Excuse me, do not talk about me as if I'm not here. I won't be foisted off on someone else. Those people are my friends and if they're in trouble, I need to help them."

"Bishop's right. You'd be safer with Eidolon or at our base. Nobody will find you and you'd be out of danger. I should have done that first, instead of bringing you here. That was a mistake and one I regret deeply."

He saw the way his words pierced her soul, inflicting a wound he didn't mean as she was taking it all wrong. He didn't regret it for the reasons she was thinking but because he'd put her in danger, and for the sake of what? His own need to see her here in his home with his family and the people he loved. He'd stopped thinking like a guard and had begun to think like a man in love and he was a fool. He'd spent his life running from commitment and love and he'd gone and fallen in love with the one woman in the world who he should be running from the hardest. In doing so, he'd gotten his mum hurt, his father kidnapped, and both their hearts broken.

"I see. Well, I'm eternally sorry your family was dragged into this mess, Justice, but I won't run from this. I ran away once and I've spent every single day since regretting my cowardice."

He heard the tremble in her voice and knew it was time to tell her the truth. "Bish, can you give us a minute?"

Bishop nodded. "I'm going to go and speak with the local PD and check on Val and Hurricane."

Reaper knew Valentina would be handling things, he'd heard her barking orders at everyone. They all thought she was laid back and sweet, but that woman had Italian blood flowing through her veins and spine of steel.

Reaper stepped toward Lucía and saw her flinch as he reached for her, his hand dropping as she raised her head like the Princess she was.

Pride filled him for the courage and bravery she was showing. "Lucía, I need to tell you something."

"Get on with it then."

He almost smiled at the haughty tone so much more befitting of her aunt, but he held it back, knowing she needed the armour. "The girl from the village, the one in the picture you took...."

Her lips wobbled as if she sensed what he was about to say. "Yes."

There was no nice way to couch this, so he gave her the words she needed. "She's dead."

Her face fell and she took an unsteady step back, her legs sagging as she sat heavily on the bed they'd left this morning full of smiles. "What?"

Reaper went to his knees and gripped her shoulders in his hands. "I wish I didn't have to tell you, angel, I really do, but it's time we face the truth."

"How did she die?"

"Her family. The shame they thought she'd brought on them was too much and they stoned her."

A gut-wrenching sob broke free, and he pulled her close, holding her as she cried for the child who should never have known such pain and suffering at anyone's hands, least of all her family's. "Why? She was innocent."

"She was engaged to the elder of another village and although the crime was against her, she was seen as damaged and therefore killed."

"God, this world is so broken."

Reaper couldn't agree more but for all the horror, she'd made him see the beauty still left in the world they lived. "It is, but it's also full of the most precious moments. You made me see that, Lucía. You made me see the beauty in the simple things, like the seconds before the sun rises and bathes the earth in light."

Her tear-stained eyes came to his and he wanted nothing more than to hold her forever, to show in every way he knew how that she was his, that he loved her, but it was all hopeless. "This is the end, isn't it?"

Reaper nodded as his heart broke and he bent to kiss her, his lips imprinting every feeling, every taste of her onto his soul. As the sweetest most life-altering kiss of his life ended, he rested his brow against hers. "I wish things were different."

The pain he could hear in her voice reflected his. "I know, so do I. I wish we had a lifetime, but we were never that."

Lucía cupped his cheek and stroked the rough skin of his beard. "Let's go and get your dad back."

Her words reminded him of the fight he faced. "Can I persuade you to go to Hereford or Longtown where it's safe?"

"I'll do whatever you need to keep us all safe and if that's Hereford or your base, then so be it. Just promise me one thing?"

"Anything."

"You end this. You make them pay for what they did."

"I will, Lucía. You have my word."

CHAPTER 21

UNCLIPPING HER SEAT BELT AS THE PRIVATE PLANE TOUCHED DOWN ON UK soil, Lucía had so many emotions going through her body and mind that she didn't know which to deal with first. Putting one foot in front of the other and maintaining an outward sense of calm when her heart was breaking in two was as much as she could do right now.

Justice had stayed away for most of the flight, giving her time to process while he handled the fine details of his father's kidnapping. Telling her not to blame herself was easy, actually doing it after the destruction that had followed her was impossible.

Valentina had stayed behind to keep an eye on Elodie, who'd been discharged and was resting at home with Caleb, John, and the kids. She understood why but she'd missed her friend more than she could say. A lifetime of only having friends who'd wanted to be seen with her because of who she was had made her put walls up but with Val, she'd found a true friend.

"We just need to secure the area before we disembark, so you have ten minutes or so, Princess Lucía."

Lucía raised a brow at Bishop as he watched as if waiting for her to fall apart. "Really? Now it's back to formalities?"

"I didn't want to assume."

"What? That we're friends? That I consider you a friend? Well, guess what, I do. So you're stuck with me and if you call me Princess again when we're alone, I'm gonna scream."

Bishop smirked. "You're the boss."

"Is it okay if I call my sister to check in with her?" Lucía was running everything by the team now. It wasn't perfect but if it kept everyone safe she'd do it.

"Sure, just don't give her details of where you are."

Lucía nodded and watched him walk away. With a smile, she took out her phone and called her sister's. Not the official one everyone knew about but her personal one that only close family had the number for.

"Hey, Lucía. I'm so happy to hear your voice."

Lucía closed her eyes and let the sound of family wash over her, easing the ache of loneliness. "Hey, sissy, how are you?"

"Don't you give me that. You got blown up and didn't call me! I've been worried sick."

"Pardon?"

Lucía glanced to Reaper who was approaching her, a heavy look on his face, and she felt such a longing it almost took her breath away. How could she spend the rest of her life loving him and not being able to be with him?

"Lucía, don't give me that. We know about the bomb at Mr Carson's house. Father has lost his mind and sent a royal protection squad to pick you up and take you to a hotel before he can bring you home."

Lucía shook her head. "That's not necessary. Justice has this in hand."

"Yes, well, Daddy doesn't think so. They should be waiting for you when you land. Go with them, Lucía."

"But...." Lucía battled with her instinct that going with the royal protection team was a bad idea, that the only person who could protect her was Justice. As she looked at his handsome face, she knew it had nothing to do with not feeling safe with the team her father had chosen, and everything to do with the fact none of them were Justice, and they never would be. It was time for her to let him go and try and move on, and this was the first step. "Okay, I'll go."

Lucía heard her sister sigh in relief and hated that she'd put so many people through hell because of one picture. She couldn't think about the reason for the image or the child or she'd fall apart and right now, she needed every ounce of control and composure she had in her arsenal.

"Thank you. Call me when you get to the hotel."

"Which is?"

"The Regent."

Lucía knew the Regent well. It was the one her father always stayed at when he was visiting for a short stay. "I'll call you when I get there."

"I love you, Lucía. Be safe."

"I love you, too."

The sisters hung up and Lucía used all her fortitude to muster up a show of strength when what she really wanted to do was cling to the man in front of her and beg him to find a way.

"I guess you heard."

Lucía stood, taking her bag, grateful she'd showered and changed into her formal attire before they'd landed. Her eyes moved to Justice, crinkles from smiling evident around his eyes, the mouth that had shown her so much pleasure was pursed now with displeasure. "I did and I think it's for the best."

"Well, I don't. Please, Lucía, stick with the plan and go with Jack and his men."

He reached for her, and she knew if he touched her, she'd crumble. Taking a slight step back she saw the pain the action caused him but there was no other way, they had to make this break clean. "I think it best if we end our association here. You need to find your father and I trust you to end this, Justice. The royal team have been vetted and have no connections to Santini or Playboy."

"I know. I'd just feel happier if you went with Jack."

God, she loved this man. Reaching out she cupped his cheek, feeling the stubble under her palm and knowing she'd never get to feel that again was a pain she'd never imagined possible. "I know, Justice. But if I've learned one thing this last few months, it's that you don't always get what you want. Be safe."

Going on tiptoes she kissed his cheek as he placed his hand over hers on his cheek, then walked toward the exit where Bishop was waiting to escort her to her car. The royal guard consisted of a four-man team who wore dark suits and had earpieces. Lucía walked to the car, sliding inside the back of the Land Rover Discovery, and sighing when the door closed. She just needed some privacy so she could have a breakdown in peace. Out of the blacked-out window, she noticed Bishop speak with the man who'd opened her door and shake his hand.

Her eyes searched for Justice and found him standing on the top steps of the plane, watching the vehicle. As if he sensed her watching him, he smiled and her heart shattered. They'd never made promises of forever yet she wanted nothing more than to be with this man. To spend her days pottering in her garden at Whitmore, taking pictures, walking with him, laughing with him, loving him. Then her sister's face came to mind, and she thought of the responsibilities she had at home, the charities, the support she had to provide and knew she couldn't walk away from her family, and her father would never permit her to marry a commoner.

The car pulled away and she refused to look back. The two men in the front of the vehicle didn't make conversation and she was glad of the protocols in place for a change. The countryside sped by, the autumn beauty giving way to the stunning desolation of winter.

It was her lack of attention that meant they made it a few miles before she figured out they weren't on their way to the Regent. Her belly flipped over, and nerves danced in her belly, her heart beating faster in her chest. "Excuse me, I was told we were going to the Regent."

"Change of plan, Ma'am. We're headed to the Langley instead. Your previous team thought it best not to repeat past behaviours and suggested a new hotel not previously used by the family."

Lucía blinked as the man in the passenger seat spoke, but his words eased her fear and it made sense that Justice would suggest that. "Fine."

"Would you like some water, Ma'am, to keep you hydrated after your long flight?"

"Yes, please."

Her throat was parched, and the cool water would help. As the man turned and handed her a bottle of sparkling water, she saw a tattoo of a chess piece on his wrist where his shirt rode up. Her eyes flew to his, sure she must be overreacting but when she saw the cold look in his eyes, she knew she wasn't.

"I guess the game is up."

The man she suspected was Chess pulled out a gun and pointed it at her as the driver smirked and carried on driving.

"Where are you taking me?" Her demand sounded haughty and confident when she felt anything but.

Chess chuckled as the driver pulled over to the side of the road. "I'm taking you home, Princess, where else?" His eyes raked over her making her skin crawl. "Then we can finish this once and for all, and you can get what you deserve."

"Justice will kill you for this."

"Justice, ha. He'll be too busy wailing over his dead father to realise, and by then it will be too late. Playboy was the perfect partner there for a while but he's no match for Reaper and he's the only one who doesn't know it. But me? I played the long game. Coming across as the accomplice when all of this was my idea. Playboy will die, the old man will die, and Reaper will be too late to save the woman he loves. Boohoo."

"You're sick."

"No, Princess, I'm a realist and money is the only power that counts. Thanks to you I almost lost my chance to be involved with Project Cradle."

Lucía had no idea what he was talking about and didn't care, she just needed to figure out how to get away.

The door was wrenched open and Lucía jumped back as the driver tried to grab her, but she kicked out, fighting for her life. She struck him in the chin, and he swore before he came at her again, but Chess already had hold of her hair through the seats. She felt the burn in her scalp before a prick of pain in her neck and then her body became unresponsive to her demands and her eyelids grew heavy before she was out.

CHAPTER 22

LOOKING AT HIS PHONE FOR THE HUNDREDTH TIME, REAPER COULDN'T SHAKE the feeling that something was very wrong. At the airport, he'd put it down to the sudden change in plans and the fact Lucía wasn't next to him. But as they drove to the address Playboy had sent him, the feeling grew stronger. This address was a secondary location and in the opposite direction of the original, heading more toward Oxford and that needled him too. Something was off and he needed to figure out what it was and fast.

"You good?"

Bás, Duchess, Lotus, Titan, and Bein had met them at the airport and now his boss was looking at him as if trying to assess his mental state.

"If you're asking if I'm okay to handle this mission, then yes."

"It's for the best, Reaper. You and Lucía wouldn't work long term."

Reaper felt his hackles go up and knew he was just jonesing for a fight. "How can you possibly know that?"

"Really? This isn't a fairy tale, Reaper. You're a highly trained operative and excellent at what you do, because of the secrecy we have that gives us protection. Do you really think you could have that married to a Princess?"

Reaper glared at Bás as if this was all his fault when he knew it was nothing but circumstance. "I could quit Shadow."

"Get your head out of your ass. You don't quit Shadow. We're family and you need this job. It's in your blood."

"I need her too." He realised he was right. He felt like he couldn't breathe without her.

"And what about her father? You really think he's going to let the likes of you marry his daughter?"

Reaper sighed because he knew Bás was right. King Juan would never agree. Lucía loved her family, and he'd never come between them. He just wished life was different. "No, I guess you're right."

Reaper glanced at Bás to see a look of disappointment on his face before he covered it.

"Good. Now let's go save your dad."

Guilt filled him that his thoughts had been so consumed by Lucía that he'd hardly given his old man a thought.

A call came through and Bás answered, putting it on speaker. "Go ahead, Jack."

"We have a huge fucking problem."

Reaper sat up, his senses screaming at him when he heard the tension in Jack's voice. "What happened?"

"We just got word Princess Lucía's entire royal protection team were found dead two hours ago by the Met."

Cold, hard dread filled his belly like lead. A ball of concrete seemed to press on his chest, stopping him from drawing air into his lungs. "We let them drive off with Lucía. Playboy has her."

"We think so too. Eidolon can handle things here. Do you need back up for your father while you find Lucía?"

A battle raged inside him, torn between going after the man who'd given him life or the woman who'd breathed life back into him. He wanted to go after Lucía, his instincts were screaming at him to do it, but his guilt was saying his dad.

"Go with your heart, Reaper."

He looked at Bás, wasting precious seconds deciding. "Yes, you get my dad. We're going after Lucía."

"On it. Keep me informed and don't fuck this up."

Jack hung up and Bás was already on a call with Duchess and the team in the second vehicle. Bishop and Hurricane, who were upfront and had been silent thus far, just nodded. The mood in the car was suddenly very different from two minutes ago as each man felt the hit of losing Lucía. He realised she hadn't just won his heart, but everyone's around her too.

"We'll get her back for you, Reaper."

Bishop's words didn't ease the pain in his chest, but they did make him sit up, determination fuelling him now. Playboy and Chess wouldn't win. He just hoped like hell he got there before they hurt her. Their sick perversions were something he couldn't think about right now or he'd puke.

Taking out his own phone he called Watchdog.

"I just heard. I'm checking the CCTV all around the airport. We're going to find them."

Knowing he didn't have to say the words or make the request, that his team was already doing everything they could and had his back, gave him renewed hope. He wished Snow was there. She was his little sister in every way but blood, but she was stuck in New York after a storm had grounded flights.

She'd found love not so long back with the Judge. He'd thought she was crazy to commit so fast but now he knew he'd leave everything he'd ever known for a chance with Lucía.

His mobile rang and he answered, hitting the speaker button. "You're on speaker, Watchdog."

"I found their car leaving the M25 at junction 25 and heading out onto the A10."

Everything began to click into place as he realised Playboy was still playing games. "He's taken her to Whitmore."

"You think he'd head there? That seems stupid to play on her turf."

Reaper nodded at Hurricane, agreeing one hundred percent. "It is but this is game to him. First, he wanted me to hand her over but then he changed his mind and snatched her. So he's going to kill her in a place she feels safe, where she has protection, to prove he can get to her anywhere and show me he's the better man."

"You sure about this?" Bás was watching him carefully.

Reaper knew this call could either save Lucía or secure her death. "Yes. It makes sense, too. He sent us toward Oxford for my father knowing that by the time I figured it out, I'd be too late. I imagine he has some elaborate call or set up to let me know it too."

"Then let's head that way."

"We should warn Jack. They might be walking into a trap."

As Bás made the call, Reaper tried to remember every detail he could about the two men behind this, every weakness, every action, every reaction that would give him the upper hand in some way. Playboy was an open book but Chess, he was more controlled, quieter and something flashed up, a memory from a different life. Of Playboy and Chess in a bar. He'd been pretty wasted himself, but it was as clear now as if a movie was playing in his head. Playboy getting in some guy's face over a woman and Chess stepping in and calming things. A few words and Playboy was under control. As if a light went on, he knew they'd been coming at this from the wrong angle. Playboy was never the lead on this, Chess was the man in charge and Playboy was just his front man. "I can't believe I missed it."

Bás, who was checking his weapons and strapping a vest into place, glanced across at him. "What do you mean?"

"Playboy isn't the one in charge, Chess is. He always has been. I just never saw it until now."

"And where has this revelation come from?"

Reaper looked toward the front seeing the other two watching him intently now too. "Chess has always been quiet in the background but looking back, he's the only person Playboy listens to. Playboy doesn't have the intelligence for this, but Chess does. He was always a good strategist and was on the team on merit, not because of who his father was."

"Well, it doesn't change a lot about how we go in, but it will once we're in there. Do you have any contacts in the village who could give us a heads up if anything is happening or has seemed odd the last few days?"

Reaper thought of all the people who loved Lucía and nodded. "Yes, let me make a call."

Ten minutes later he was off the phone with a very annoyed Mrs Howard, who was concerned about the potholes getting worse because of people in big cars, but she'd given him more than that. "Mrs Howard says that Mr Jonson in the post office saw four men hanging around old Mr Cradley's farm. He died last year, and his family haven't gone through probate, so it's abandoned. When he confronted them, they said they were surveying it for sale, but he didn't believe them."

"Then that's where they're going."

Reaper shook his head, his brain spinning in ten different directions as they came up to the sign advising Whitmore was three miles out. "I'm not sure. Yes, I think they're holed up there, but I think they'll take Lucía to her cottage. They'll want to rub my nose in it."

Bás stowed his secondary pistol in a leg holster and shrugged. "Then we cover both."

He dialled the number for Duchess as Reaper mentally prepared for what he might find when he got there. He was trying to be an optimist but if he wasn't prepared in some way, he'd jeopardise Lucía and his teammates. Even the thought of the woman he knew he loved with those two made him shudder inside, but he locked it down.

He needed to control his emotions, not let them control him or he'd never get out of there safely. He'd always thought his nickname was a joke, not seeing what others did when they looked at him. A man happy to walk the line of death with life beside him, his willingness to go to any lengths wasn't something he really considered but now he knew he didn't just walk the line. In this moment, and for Playboy and Chess and any other man in his way, he was death and he was coming for them.

CHAPTER 23

HER BODY JOLTED AS SHE HIT SOMETHING SOFT, WAKING HER FROM THE unconscious state she'd fallen into. A gasp tore from her lips and Lucía began to fight the ties at her wrists as memories flooded her. Voices behind her made her turn and as she did, the room came properly into focus and confusion speared through her brain when she recognised her cottage.

"Welcome back, Princess."

The gravelly voice held a sneer which made her skin crawl as she wriggled her body to look at the man speaking behind her. With her arms and legs tied it was almost impossible, but she wouldn't have her back to him.

Fear leeched into her blood like poison as she faced the man who'd been hunting her. On the outside, he was handsome in a clean-cut way, but she'd seen the cruelty in him when he'd attacked that poor girl and knew his beauty was superficial. He had a black heart full of hate and evil.

"Why have you brought me here?" Her demand made him smile but she needed to control the narrative as much as she could and buy herself time for Justice to find her. And he would, she knew he would. Her tiny bolthole of a home, which encompassed the real her in more ways than any other place she'd lived, was being desecrated by these monsters.

Her eyes moved away from the man smirking at her to see the other one, Chess, watching them closely. Her furniture had been broken, trinkets she'd collected from around the world smashed, and books torn to pieces.

"What? Don't you like it here?"

Lucía glared at him from her seat on her once loved couch. A place that held so many happy memories for her over the years and more importantly, of Justice and her sharing meals.

Ignoring Playboy, she looked to Chess. "What do you want from me?"

He cocked his head, intelligent eyes watching her. He wasn't handsome or ugly, but the coldness in his eyes made her shiver. He was the biggest threat to her life here.

"You put everything I've been working for in danger. I need you to die, but first I need something from you."

"You're crazy if you think Justice or my father will let you get away with this. You're dead men walking."

A cry tore through her as Playboy grabbed a handful of her hair and wrenched her head back. "The only people dead will be you and that boyfriend of yours, bitch."

His face was so close she could see the red flecks in his eyes and knew he was on drugs. Lucía recognised the signs from her time with the charities. Playboy sniffed before he lowered his head and licked her neck, the action making her gag, his warm breath and tongue on her such an invasion. But she knew it could get so much worse and vowed not to show him her fear.

"That's enough, Playboy. You'll get your turn when I have my money."

Playboy caressed her cheek with the barrel of his gun and shoved her away, making her fall back onto the couch, her elbow twisting painfully behind her.

Struggling again, she sat up and faced her captors. "What money? I thought this was about the picture I took." Her eyes darted around, trying to find some way of escape or a weapon she could use, but nothing was close enough.

Chess moved to look out of the window, pulling the blinds back a little so he could see. Turning back, he looked at Playboy and motioned with the semi-automatic weapon he was holding. "Go check the back and make sure it's secure, then bring the stuff into this room."

Playboy frowned. "Let the grunts do it."

Lucía watched the power dynamic between the two men and saw cracks she might be able to exploit.

"I said check the fucking back, Playboy." Chess looked angry but relaxed his expression and changed his tone at Playboy's obvious building anger. "Please. I don't trust them, but I know I can trust you."

"Fine, but I'm having a smoke while I'm out there."

"That's okay, just watch your six."

"Always do, my man." Playboy disgustingly grabbed his crotch and laughed as he made a thrusting motion at her. "Back soon, bitch. Then we can play."

Lucía watched Chess move a kitchen chair into the middle of the room and felt her belly knot tight. Not giving in to fear would be the hardest thing she'd done but she had to fight, for her family and for Justice. That man would blame himself for eternity if she died.

"What do you want from me?"

Chess strolled over to her and gently took her arm, hoisting her into a standing position. He led her toward the chair and sat her down with a push, before going behind her and cutting the ties on her wrists. "Don't do anything stupid."

"I won't." If compliance got her hands free from the ties, she'd take it.

Coming around the front of the chair, he leaned down and reached a hand to her belly. "I need you to grow me some nice healthy babies in here for a few years, then you can die. From what I hear, you'll be begging for death. But first, we have to get that idiot Reaper to think you're dead."

The calm with which he spoke sent a chill down her spine, but it was the words that made her heart beat so hard she thought she might die from it. Lucía moved to flee, her fight or flight reaction choosing flight, but she forgot her ankles were tied together and fell to the ground at Chess' feet. A dark rumble of laughter filled the room, and she knew she'd reacted exactly as he'd expected. Tears bit her eyes and she furiously blinked them back. She wouldn't give him the satisfaction of seeing her cry.

His hands were rough this time as he dragged her to the seat again and secured her hands in front of her.

"That was silly. I had considered keeping you from Playboy and only allowing the insemination to be a medical procedure, but my boy deserves some fun."

The thought of Playboy or anyone other than Justice touching her filled her mouth with bile. "Why are you doing this?"

"The company I'm working with are breeding sleepers. Those kids will be the finest soldiers in history. Have the best education, unique and innovative training, and the most ground-breaking fitness and health techniques will be used. They'll be the greatest assets the world has ever seen. Nobody will be able to beat them, they'll be killing machines. And the real beauty is that when they're out there in the world, nobody will suspect a thing. They'll have ordinary lives until they're activated."

Lucía reared back in horror at what he was suggesting and even more so that he believed what he was saying. "You can't be serious? You'd bring these kids up in a mini army and train them to kill?"

"They'll have the very best and their fee will be the work they do when asked."

"What about the mothers and fathers?"

"You have to break some eggs to make an omelette, Princess. The fathers will be elite soldiers chosen by the doctors, and the mothers are either runaways or drug addicts with no other choice. We're helping those women."

Her emotions were running hot as she fought to understand how anyone could think this was okay. "You're taking their babies."

"Babies they can't look after. Do you know what it's like to grow up poor, with no money for food? Wearing clothes with holes in them because your mother stuck the money you needed for food or clothing in her veins?"

A kernel of sympathy seeded its way into her, and she shook her head. "No, I don't, but this isn't the way."

"It is, and it gets me a life I never imagined when I was sitting in that crack house watching my mother die."

"What about me? I'm not a runaway or a drug addict."

"No, you're my ticket to the good life. With your breeding and an elite solider as the father, I'll get top dollar and the threat of that photo off my back."

"It's not you in the photo. You could walk away."

Chess shook his head. "No, Playboy saved me when we were kids, offered me friendship and a way out of the system. I couldn't walk away from him."

"But you don't approve of what he does?"

Chess cocked his head to look at the door behind her. "Playboy has something broken inside him. He needs to do the things he does. It's a sickness. I just help him control it so he stays off the radar and when I can't, his father or Godfather does."

"Except the last time when he couldn't, and you both got booted for it."

Chess's jaw twitched as he glared at her. "He's getting harder to handle, but this payday will free me."

"Then you'll, what? Walk away?"

He shook his head and she saw genuine sadness on his face. "No, I'll end it."

Lucía watched him look behind her as the door opened and

Playboy stomped back inside with a tripod and camera in his hands which he began to set up.

"So, you fake my death and sell me to these people to breed me and then they kill me?"

Playboy shot his finger at her. "Got it in one, baby, but in between, me and you are gonna have some fun."

"You disgust me." Lucía spat in his face knowing she'd earn his wrath and hoping it would cause a fight between him and Chess. Chess was about money and a new life, but Playboy liked the violence.

"You whore." Playboy lunged and Chess caught him around the chest and sent her a glare.

"Calm the fuck down."

Playboy rounded on him. "Did you see what that bitch did? She needs to pay."

"Later, man, okay?"

"No. Fuck later. She pays now."

Playboy lunged again and she tried to scoot back but before he got to her, Playboy staggered, shock in his eyes. As he turned accusing eyes on his friend, she saw the knife in his back as Chess withdrew the blade and plunged it into his heart.

A scream died in her throat as Playboy fell, holding his chest and Chess caught him and eased him to the ground, cradling his body.

"I'm sorry, brother, but this needed to end. You're sick and I couldn't help you anymore."

The grief in the man's voice was palpable and Lucía knew in some way she was responsible for the horror in front of her.

Silently she watched as Chess lifted Playboy's body from the ground and laid him on her couch before he straightened. "You did that. You look at him and know that was you, not me. You forced my hand, and it wasn't pretty. I'm going to make sure you get to watch when I kill Reaper."

Tears slid freely down her face, but she made no sound, lost in her own shock and fear. Chess set the camera up and pointed it at her before quickly moving back to the window and checking outside again. "You have very nosey neighbours. It's gonna get them killed."

Lucía closed her eyes choking back the cry as she heard Mr Jonson whistling as he approached her door. "Please don't hurt him."

Chess looked back at her. "You going to be compliant?"

"Yes. I'll do what you ask." Lucía would for now to save her friend, and she prayed Justice found her before it was too late.

CHAPTER 24

"WHAT THE FUCK IS HE DOING?"

Reaper watched Mr Jonson stroll towards Lucía's front door, whistling as if he hadn't a care in the world. The team had arrived on foot five minutes earlier and scoped out the area. Two men were situated out the back and two more in the village. Playboy had come out the back and it had taken every bit of control he had not to put a bullet between his eyes, but he'd known it was a mistake.

"Fuck knows, but he needs to get the fuck out of there before he ends up as collateral in this mess, or worse, gets Lucía killed."

Bishop was beside him; they were split into two teams now. Hurricane, Duchess, and Bishop were with him, and Bás, Bein, and Lotus were clearing the village. They were waiting on word from Jack and his men, deciding the best time to attack was a direct timed assault so that no one could warn the others.

The wait was torture knowing Lucía was so close and he couldn't get to her yet.

Through the scope, Reaper saw the door open and then a blessed sighting of the woman he loved. She was still dressed in the clothes from the plane. Her hair was down and messed as if she'd been grabbed but she seemed unhurt and to him, she was the most beautiful sight in the world.

Her eyes darted around and as if sensing him, she looked toward the hedgerow and seemed to stare for a split second before turning back to Mr Jonson.

"Hey, Mr Jonson, what can I do for you?"

Her voice was clear and louder than needed, but he expected she was talking louder for his benefit.

"Lucía, have you seen these strangers in the village? I thought you should know in case they're paparazzi."

"Yes, I had heard. I'm going to lie low for a day or so until they leave."

"Yes, well, you do look a little tired, my dear. Can I get you anything? Food supplies, some of Mrs Jonson's soup and cookies?"

"That sounds lovely, but can we leave it until tomorrow? The flight has exhausted me, and I think I might get an early night."

Mr Jonson nodded, but Reaper was watching her hand. She was trying to sign something with one hand.

"Shit. I had no idea she knew ASL, and I can't understand what she's saying."

"I can," Bishop responded beside him. "She's saying Playboy is dead and one man inside."

"Fuck. That means Chess killed him."

"Yep, and that ain't good because he's coming up on his end game."

They continued to watch until Mr Jonson walked away and Lucía disappeared behind the closed door.

A bleep came through the comm, and he pressed the button on his wristwatch, expecting Jack or Bás but it was neither.

"Okay, I've been digging, and I found bank accounts for Micah Rawlings aka Chess in the Cayman Islands. There's two million dollars in there."

"Okay." Reaper wasn't sure how significant or time-sensitive this

was but kept listening, knowing Watchdog wouldn't call unless it was important.

"Yeah, here's the kicker. The payments have been ten equal lump sums over the last eighteen months from a shell corporation called Styles Inc. That means nothing on its own, but after digging further I found that Joel Hansen is on the board of directors."

Reaper looked at Bishop and Hurricane, knowing this was big. They'd been after Hansen for a long time now and this was a huge lead.

"So, I guess you don't want this fucker dead, Bás?"

"Affirmative, we need him alive, but Lucía's safety comes first."

"Roger that."

"I'll keep digging."

"Yeah. Look into Cradle. This is linked to that."

"Will do."

The line went dead, and Reaper waited, each second feeling like hours when in fact it was no more than two minutes since he'd seen the woman he loved in the flesh.

"Boss man in position. On my go."

Reaper felt his muscles bunch in readiness, the adrenalin already flooding his body as he prepared to infiltrate the place that had become a second home to him. He heard the rest of the team check-in from their various positions then silence before, *"Execute, execute, execute."*

He, Bishop, and Hurricane were on their feet moving swiftly around the side of the hedge, where they split. He and Hurricane moved toward the back to clear the men patrolling, and Bishop went towards the side, where a door led to the garden.

The deep brambled hedges gave them cover as Hurricane took out the first man clean and he dropped the second one. Their surprise now gone, they began to take fire and had to pull back slightly.

As a unit with one mind, he and Hurricane pushed forward again, taking careful, well-placed shots instead of raining the countryside in bullets, the heads of the late-blooming Dahlia's Lucía loved exploding from gunfire. The early sunset was helping as the low light gave them more cover.

"Sit rep, Bish?"

The silence that greeted him filled his gut with dread.

"Hurricane, can you handle this?"

"Yep, you go."

Reaper ducked left taking the path down the side of the house as Hurricane dealt with the last man. The side door was open, and he checked the two rooms he passed, finding both clear before he headed for the main room.

Rounding the corner, he felt his jaw clench with anger as he took in the situation. Bishop was on his knees near the couch, Lucía tied to a chair in the centre. Chess had a gun aimed at her head and another aimed at Bishop.

He cast a glance at his friend and saw Playboy's dead body bleeding into the cream sofa.

"You don't have to do this, Chess."

"You're a fucking idiot, Reaper. I'm leaving this house and taking this bitch with me."

"I can't let you do that."

"You can and you will. Now, put your weapon down before I kill her here and now."

"You kill her, you die too. You know that."

Chess shook his head. "No, you won't risk her life."

Chess cocked the weapon he was holding and wrenched Lucía's head back on her neck, making her wince but she didn't cry out or move.

Rage swept through him but not a volatile, out-of-control feeling. No, this was cold and deadly and promised pain to the man in front of him. "Fine. I'm putting my gun down. Just don't hurt her." He glanced at Lucía who was watching him, her teeth biting into her lip as she glanced down and up and then did it again. Following her eye line, he saw wires running around the front door leading to her chair. His gut hitched as he realised Chess had rigged the house to blow.

"Why don't you let Lucía go and we can talk about this? See if we can find a way out."

Chess laughed, "You must think I'm fucking stupid. There's no way you're going to let me walk away from this. You're death remember, and it always comes for you, no matter how long you run."

"Then you know I'll find you no matter how hard you try to hide."

"Not if you're dead."

"You're surrounded, Chess. You know there's no play for you. You lose."

Chess looked at Bishop and then him before he seemed to realise what Reaper said was right. "Always so clever weren't you, Reaper? Thinking you were the best. So moral and clean when you had the most kills of all the men I knew."

"You're right. I did kill a lot of people, but the difference between you and me is that I don't enjoy the kill. I do it because it's necessary."

"Sure, that's why you got yourself out of the military and got a cushy gig with this lot."

"I was kicked out of the military because of you and Playboy."

"Kill or be killed, right, Reaper? You know that, and I had to protect my boy."

Reaper glanced at Playboy. "Yeah, so you could kill him."

Chess went still, his face red with anger, body tense and Reaper knew it was time for the kill. "So, what now?"

"I'm going to leave here with Lucía and you're going to die in a horrible explosion. By the time your team figures out what happened, I'll be long gone, and she'll be in the stable with the other broodmares."

Hearing him talk about Lucía like that made him want to rip his heart out. Only the tiniest movement from the window made him pause from the attack he was about to launch. Readying his body, he waited for a second until Hurricane was in position outside, the comm in his ear giving him an advantage which somehow Chess had failed to see. As he gave the order, Hurricane fired the bullet hitting Chess in the throat. As he fell, Reaper dove for Lucía who screamed.

Reaper wrapped her in his arms as she shook. "It's okay, it's okay."

He kissed her cheek, before raising his head and saw the dead man's switch in Chess' left hand that Hurricane had warned him about over comms. Chess reached for his throat with his free hand to stop the blood, as he held tight to the switch, knowing he could blow himself to smithereens if he let go as his breath gurgled in his airway.

CHAPTER 25

CHAOS FILLED THE ROOM AS HURRICANE RUSHED THROUGH THE FRONT DOOR. The scent of blood and the sound of gurgling came at her as if through a tunnel.

"Lucía, angel, look at me."

She turned her head in a daze following the sound of Justice's voice as he laid a hand on her cheek guiding her to look at him. His face was tender yet focused and she blinked to try and get her bearings, the horror of the last few hours suddenly hitting her, and it wasn't over.

"I need you to stay still for me while I disarm this bomb, okay? Can you do that for me?"

Lucía looked around and saw Bishop kneeling beside her and Hurricane hovering over Chess, stemming the bleeding from his neck wound.

"Okay."

"Good girl."

She saw him give Bishop a look of worry and knew it was because of her. She was falling apart at the worst possible time, and she needed to get it together and help these men or they could all die and she couldn't allow that to happen.

"Reaper, I'm going to take the switch from Chess so Hurricane can get him out of here and into the ambulance."

"You sure you want to do that?" The warning in Reaper's voice as he asked Bishop the question amplified how dire the situation was.

"Don't be a dick. Of course I'm sure. I'm not leaving you or Lucía, so you just get to diffusing this bomb, 'cos I've got my ex-wife blowing up my phone and if I don't answer, she gets all snippy."

Reaper nodded and got to work once Bishop secured the switch in his own fist. She'd known when Chess had begun to assemble the wires around the chair that this was how he was going to confuse people about her fake death. Her belly was in knots as she tried not to panic, but the reality was they could all die now, and she didn't want that.

"You should go. I don't want anyone dying for me."

Reaper cocked a brow at her. "I'm wounded that you don't have faith in me, angel."

His wink made her heart skid to halt before it galloped away in her chest. "I trust you, Justice. I just can't bear the thought of anything happening to you or Bishop."

"Nothing is going to happen to any of us." Reaper gave his friend another look, and an unspoken communication seemed to take place.

"Lucía, did I ever tell you about my she-devil ex-wife?"

Despite the situation, the description of his ex-wife made her smile. "No, what was she like?"

Bishop shook his head before he, too, smiled. "Fucking annoying as hell. She had the coldest feet you've ever heard of. It was a miracle those lumps of ice didn't fall off. She was also stubborn as hell, and boy, when she went off, you didn't want to be in the same postcode. She had a temper worse than a rattlesnake and the skills to use it."

"She sounds terrifying."

"She is, but she's the best operative I've ever worked with. She had an intuition about things that was almost spooky. She used to know exactly when I needed her when we worked together, said she could feel it."

It was clear as day to Lucía that Bishop was still head over heels for his ex-wife. "You still love her."

"Hell no. She tried to kill me."

"She must have had her reasons. I don't believe two people with that kind of connection would simply betray each other."

"Neither did I but she shot me and left me for dead. The next thing I heard was divorce papers landing on my doorstep." Bishop had a reflective look on his face, and she could see the pain her betrayal had caused him.

"Yet you still have contact with her?"

"A necessary evil. As I said, she's a good operator and from an intel perspective, she's the best. So I keep in touch for that reason."

"Did she ever tell you why she shot you and left?"

Bishop shook his head. "Nah, and I never asked."

"Really, Noah, you still bitching about that?"

Lucía looked to the door at the same time as Bishop to see a tall, beautiful woman leaning against the doorjamb. Her athletic frame was dressed in skin-tight jeans, a white round neck tee, and a black denim jacket. Her golden blonde hair was in a long ponytail that curled around her neck. Arms folded across her chest, she gave Bishop an annoyed look with her wide green eyes and her full lips pursed.

"Charlie, what the hell are you doing here?"

Lucía had guessed but it was nice to get confirmation on her identity.

Charlie strolled forward, casting a glance and small smile at Lucía as she peered at Reaper, who was sliding out from beneath the chair. "Well, you sent a text asking for my help then failed to answer my calls. I thought I should head your way and find out what messed up shit you've got yourself into this time."

Turning to Lucía, she held out her hand and then noticed her

179

hands were still zip-tied and took out a small flick knife and cut through the plastic. Blood rushed back into her wrists and Lucía rubbed them, grateful to be free.

"Charlie Pope, nice to meet you. Don't believe a word he says about me. He's like a bitter teen who got dumped at prom."

"Lucía. It's very nice to meet you too." She angled her head. "Did you shoot him?"

"Oh yeah, that bit's true. But you've met him, right?"

"Charlie, you can't just turn up when you feel like it."

As Bishop and Charlie took their argument outside, Justice came around to untie her legs, his hands gentle as they touched her.

"You're safe now, angel."

Suddenly feeling awkward now that the danger was over, she didn't know what to do. Lucky for her Justice did, and he took her in his arms and held her tight as if he'd never let go.

"Thank you." The words weren't enough. They'd never be enough, but they were all she had.

All too soon he was pulling back to look at her. "Did they hurt you?" His tone was deep and pained and she could only imagine what was going through his mind.

"No, Chess wouldn't let Playboy touch me and he killed him before he could."

Justice glanced toward the couch. "He was sick. Death was the only way for a man like him."

Lucía nodded and took the hand he offered as he helped her to stand. Her legs wobbled and before she knew it, she was in his arms as he carried her into the dusky darkness that had descended, heading for the ambulance. He set her down and stepped back so the paramedics could take a look, but he stayed close in case she needed him. The place was now swarming with Shadow team members, and she realised this wasn't a regular ambulance and wondered who it belonged to. "Who do you work for?"

The paramedic gave her a look and ignored her question as he asked her a bunch of questions about the attack and any injuries she might have sustained before finishing his checks.

Justice walked toward her and crouched next to her, his hand on her knee as he slid his fingers through hers. "Your father is on his way. Hurricane and Bás are going to stay with you until he gets here. You're safe now, Lucía."

"But why can't you stay with me?" Her breathing felt panicked now at the thought of him leaving her.

Justice closed his eyes and dropped his head to her thigh, his breathing fast as if he was trying hard to hold onto his control. When he looked up again, she saw the desperation and emotion in his eyes, and it almost broke her. "I wish I could, but he wants me off the case. He blames me and he's right. I left you open to attack and failed to protect you."

"No, you couldn't have known."

"Yes, Lucía, I should have. It's my job to know, to predict, and I should have realised it was Chess and that taking you home would be an obvious choice to them. I was selfish because I wanted to be with you and show you my home and my family, and it almost cost you your life. So, yes, it's my fault."

Lucía could feel the tears sliding down her cheeks and knew she'd never convince him he was wrong and to what end, they still had no future. He lived for his job. It was his life, and he was good at it. She knew he saved hundreds of lives with what he did. She could never jeopardise that by thrusting him into the limelight that was her life. But she couldn't leave her family either, and her father would never forgive her if she walked away.

Running her hand through his soft hair, she tried to bank every second of her time with him knowing she'd never love another man as she did him. Leaning in she kissed his cheek. "I'll always love you, Justice, and I won't ever forget you."

His groan was torn from him as he cupped her face and kissed her hard, pouring all his feelings into it. A flame of desire licked up her spine but was overshadowed by love and despair at the thought of never having this again. Justice consumed her—his scent, his taste, all of her belonged to him. Then he was pulling away on a gritty moan and striding away from her as she cried for what could've been and what would never be again.

A hand on her shoulder had her turning to see Charlie standing beside her, a look of sympathy on her face. "Men, can't live with them, can't kill them."

Lucía laughed through her tears. "And you should know, you tried."

Charlie went still and then she was laughing. Seconds later Lucía's laughter turned to tears as she sobbed uncontrollably. Comforting arms wrapped around her, and she heard the murmured words of comfort this woman was bestowing on her. She clung to the hope that one day she'd get over the loss of the man who'd stolen her heart.

CHAPTER 26

"Can you believe our girl is getting married?"

Reaper was standing at the bar inside the hotel where Snow was about to marry the Judge, having a drink with Duchess, Bein, Lotus, Titan, and Watchdog. Hurricane and Bishop were with Rykov, talking to the groom who looked as nervous as a cat in a room full of rocking chairs.

Shaking his head, he glanced at Duchess who'd posed the question. She was wearing the same colour dresses as the other bridesmaids, and they all looked beautiful. Not that anyone could hold a candle to Lucía. His gut tightened with familiar pain as it always did when she slipped past the barrier he'd created for her.

He missed every single thing about her, from her smile, to her heart, to the way she'd cross her legs and tuck her ankles like the queen she was inside. He also missed the feel of her hands on him, the way she tasted when he kissed her, and the way she could make him laugh at the silliest things.

His mother's burgers were ruined, the memory of making them with her that first time too much to bear. Every day he got up and punished his body with a brutal workout, pushing himself so that he was better, faster, more focused as if that could erase the mistakes of the past.

He'd spoken to his father and mother, as well as Caleb, and his mum and brother were helping his dad through the end of his life. The rescue to save his father, carried out by Eidolon had been straight forward. With only four men holding his father at Chess' command, it had been an easy take down for the team. No loss of life and those men were now in custody awaiting charges. He planned to travel back to Australia in January so he could lay eyes on his mother and hug her and thank her, and just because even as old as he was, he missed her.

Chess had survived the shot from Hurricane and Reaper knew it had been a choice to shoot him in the neck not the head and which side. Hurricane had spotted the dead man's switch and alerted him over the comms just before the shot was taken, thank God, or this would be a very different day for them all.

Chess was in a secure facility awaiting trial for kidnapping and murder and would, without doubt, go down for the rest of his life if he lived long enough to get there. He'd given them nothing more than what he'd told Lucía about Cradle and the network of sleepers they were building. It was enough though because it was a piece of the puzzle and connected to Hansen, giving them leads they hadn't had before. It would most likely earn Chess a painful death in prison, but he didn't have it in him to care.

Hansen, though, was a real bastard. Bás had a personal grudge with the man but nobody knew what it was, and he didn't volunteer details which was okay. They all had their secrets.

His brow furrowed as he thought of the elaborate funeral Playboy had received and the lies told to cover up how he'd died. He knew bitterness wouldn't do him any good, but in his book, justice hadn't been served. He'd died easy and quick, but at least he was no longer a threat to anyone.

"You still in a funk over Lucía?"

Reaper realised it was just him and Duchess now, the others joining the groom while he'd been deep in thought. "I'm fine."

"Are you? Because from what I can see, you're killing yourself."

Reaper angled a glare at his boss and a woman he respected. "No offence but didn't you tell me to end it?"

Duchess shook her head, her dark hair brushing the tattoos she wore with pride. "No, I didn't say that. My words were, Princess Lucía is in love with you and if I'm not very much mistaken the feeling is mutual, and if not, you need to end it right now. But it's painfully clear that it's mutual and you do love her."

Reaper pushed his fingers through his hair in frustration. "What do you want me to say, Duchess? That I love her more than anything in this world? That every second without her feels like I'm dying a slow, painful death? That I can't sleep because I dream of her and then I wake up and she isn't there?" He paced away and faced her again as she watched him carefully.

"Then why don't you fight for her?"

"How? She's a fucking Princess for God's sake and her father hates my guts. I'd never come between her and the family she loves."

"Don't you think that's up to her to decide?"

"It makes no difference. She'll never see me again after I broke her damn heart and walked away for a second time."

"Maybe." Duchess shrugged and walked away as the bridal party began to get into position.

Reaper finished his drink and headed toward the room where Snow would marry Sebastian. Walking to the front, he took a seat beside Hurricane and behind Jack and his wife, Astrid. They exchanged pleasantries, Reaper knowing how much it would mean to Snow that Jack had come. The man had saved them all in his way, and none of them would ever be able to repay him for what he'd given them.

Sebastian caught his eye from the front where he was waiting for Snow to appear, his brow peppered with sweat and he knew the man loved Snow and would protect her with his life. Giving the man a chin lift, he acknowledged this and then all eyes moved to the back of the room as the music began to play.

He couldn't tear his eyes from the woman who was sitting four rows back on the opposite side beside Bishop though. Lucía looked as gut-wrenchingly beautiful as he remembered, perhaps even more so. Her head turned and their eyes locked as if there was nobody else in the room but them. The air seemed to still and the pull of her almost overwhelmed him.

Their eyeline was broken as the bridesmaids walked past, little Fleur looking every inch the angel she was, followed by Val, Duchess, and Lotus. His eyes found hers again and she smiled, looking shy and unsure, an ethereal quality about the way she stood made him wonder if he hadn't lost his damn mind and was imagining her.

Then Snow walked past, and he pulled his focus to the woman who was like a sister to him as Bás gave her away to the man who every single one of them had threatened with bodily harm if he hurt her. He may have had his doubts about Sebastian but as he looked at Snow with tears in his eyes, every single one of them vanished.

As the ceremony progressed, he kept looking back to see Lucía watching him, only to look away when he caught her. It became a game and he smiled at her the last time, and she grinned back, and it was if all his wishes came true at once.

As the ceremony finished and Snow and Seb walked back up the aisle, he lost Lucía in the crowd. When he found her, she was in the bar with Valentina and Bishop as the happy couple had photos taken in the freezing snow.

"Lucía."

"Hello, Justice."

God, the sound of his name on her lips made him ache. "What are you doing here?" Jealousy at seeing her standing beside Bishop made him want to punch his friend out.

"Val asked me as her plus one and I said yes. I hope you don't mind."

"God, no. Why would I?"

Lucía shrugged and his attention was drawn to the deep emerald Bardot neck dress she was wearing and the cleavage it hinted at. "I don't know."

He had so many things he wanted to say to her and no idea where to start. Bishop and Val wandered off, with his friend winking at him. "You look so damn beautiful."

Her blush reminded him of all the times he'd given her compliments and she'd done the same thing.

"You look very handsome, too."

Reaper looked down at the tux he wore and shrugged. "I feel like a damn penguin."

She laughed, the husky sound burning into his soul and he wondered how he'd ever live without her and realised he couldn't, and he didn't want to. Did she feel the same? Could she by some miracle still love him, or had it been an illusion?

"Reaper, we need you."

He turned to see Snow calling him and remembered it was her day, and he wouldn't do anything to ruin it or take the focus from her. "I need to go. Are you staying so we can talk?"

She nodded, the drink in her hand wobbling bringing his eyes down her body and making his own harden in response.

"Yes, I'm staying if that's okay."

"More than okay."

He grinned and rushed off to get his duties done so he could get back to the woman who was watching him as she laughed with Watchdog and Bishop. Despite his best efforts, he didn't find a single second to speak with Lucía until after dinner and by then his mood was as sour as shit. It felt like everything was conspiring to stop him from getting to her. First the pictures, then the meal, then the speeches, then Fleur, who he couldn't be mad at because she was too adorable. Now, though, he didn't care if the world imploded, he was having his time with Lucía and God help any person who got in his way.

Walking up to her, he dragged her away from Valentina, Bein, and Aoife and onto the dance floor where Seb and Snow had just invited people to join them. On the dance floor, he pulled her into his arms, and it was as if everything settled into place. His world was the right way up again—finally.

Her soft body settled against his much harder one and he held her close, her hair tickling his nose, her scent so familiar and seductive he knew she'd be able to feel his hard cock against her belly. "God, I've missed this."

Lucía held herself away as she looked up at him, her eyes wide and heavy with desire. "I've missed you, too."

She wanted to say more, he could hear her unspoken condemnation for leaving her and it made his throat close with regret. "I'm sorry for hurting you."

Lucía blinked, her smile falling and he knew he was getting this wrong. "Are you?"

"Yes, of course. I never should have gotten involved."

"Really, Justice, that's what you want to say to me after all these weeks? That you're sorry you hurt me?"

"It's the truth. What else do you want me to say?"

"Maybe that you love me, and you feel like every second without me is like a blade through your heart. That you can't live without me."

Reaper saw the pain he was causing her, and words failed him again. He did feel all that, but it wasn't even half of what he felt.

"Forget it. This was a mistake."

Lucía wrenched from his arms and ran for the exit, and it took him a second to wrap his head around what was happening.

Bishop shook his head. "God damn, and I thought I was stupid."

His words snapped him out of the funk he was in, and he gave chase. He couldn't let her walk away from him again not ever. As he got to the front of the hotel, he saw her waiting for her coat and reached for her arm. "Lucía, wait. Please?"

She rounded on him then and the sight of tears running down her face gutted him.

"Go away, Justice."

He pulled her by her arm, casting his eyes around for somewhere private and found a door leading to a cleaning cupboard. Once inside, he closed the door and flicked the switch, giving him a small amount of light to see her. "I can't do that."

Lucía sniffed and held herself stiff, her wrist still in his grip and he released her. Before she could move away, he gripped her hips and crowded her against the wall. The hitch in her breath proved she was as affected as he was by their proximity.

"Of course you can. It's what you do, isn't it? Walk away without a goodbye."

"It was, yes, and then I met this amazing woman who changed my life. She showed me that I was only half living before her. That life is about taking chances, not just with my body but with my heart."

He stroked her hair back from her face and trailed his fingers down her throat, feeling the pulse in her neck pounding as hard as his heart was. "I love you, Lucía. God knows I didn't plan to, but meeting you was the best thing to ever happen to me. You're the other half of my soul, the light to my darkness, and I don't want to spend a single second more without you by my side."

"You love me?"

Reaper laughed then. "Love seems such a weak word for what I feel but, yes. I love and adore you."

"Can we make this work, Justice? I can't leave my family. It's not like I can quit and I'd never ask you to leave Shadow. They're as much your family as mine is to me."

"We'll find a way because I can't live without you and if I have to leave Shadow to be with you, then that's what I'll do."

"No, I couldn't ask that."

"You're not asking. I love you, Lucía. You're my life now, and if you want me, I'll spend every day making sure you don't regret falling for an idiot like me."

"Never. I love you, Justice. I think I have from that first day."

"Good. Now come here."

He kissed her slow and lazily, his hands cupping her neck and her ass as he pulled her close. His body remembered every curve and dip of her sexy body. Desire hit like an earthquake and suddenly he was frenzied, the need to be inside her making him crazy. Her soft moans and whimpers as he kissed his way down her neck threatened his control, his hands pushing the top of her dress down so he could see her perfect tits.

"Christ, you're beautiful." As he dipped his head to suck one gorgeous nipple into his mouth through the lace, he felt her hands at his zipper.

"I need you inside me."

His cock ached it was so hard for her as he dragged her skirt up, his fingers finding the lace of her underwear soaked through for him. "Goddammit, you're so wet for me."

His mouth found hers as he stroked through her flesh, making her arch against him searching for more. He filled her with two fingers, pushing inside her tight body and making them both groan. His thumb ran over her clit, and he fucked her with his hand until she fell apart, his mouth catching her cry of pleasure as his body took the weight of hers when her legs gave way.

Pulling his hand away he sucked his fingers into his mouth and moaned, low and deep at the taste of her, so sweet.

"Fuck me, Justice."

Lifting her, he bunched her skirt and released his cock from his trousers and thrust inside her in one quick movement. Reaper stilled as he realised he'd taken her with no protection.

"It's fine. I'm on the pill."

Relief made him sigh and lust took over and he was holding her against the wall as he fucked her hard. Hands and mouths a frenzy of movement as he felt her begin to shake around his cock, her body tightening in that familiar way that preceded her climax. This time she took him with her, and he growled his release as pleasure like he'd never known before blasted through his spine leaving him weak.

As they both came down from their life-changing releases, he set her feet on the ground and straightened her clothes before he did the same. He didn't let her go though. He didn't know if he ever would again.

As he zipped up his trousers the door behind him opened wide and a giggling Bein and Aoife stood there. When they saw them, their jaws dropped in shock before Bein slammed the door.

Looking to Lucía he waited for her response and knew it was all going to be okay when she burst out laughing. "Oh. My. God."

Her hands covered her face as she giggled, and he wrapped her in his arms, content to stay here for eternity as long as she was here too.

EPILOGUE

Reaper took a deep breath and knocked on the door, the elaborate crest of the royal family displayed with pride.

"Come in."

Reaper opened the door knowing the King was expecting him and hoping like hell this went the way he hoped because he was doing it anyway. Nerves worse than any pre-combat concern tightened his chest. He wondered if this was how he died, asking the father of the woman he loved for her hand in marriage.

"Justice, what can I do for you?"

The King motioned for the chair after Justice dropped a bow to the man who ruled this country.

He waited until the King sat and took the chair opposite him. They'd come to a grudging understanding since Lucía had made it clear Justice was in her life to stay.

"Firstly, I want to apologise for not protecting Lucía as well as I should have. It's unforgivable and I understand why you hate me."

"I do not hate you. I was angry. My baby girl had been kidnapped and endangered and I was worried sick and lashing out. That said, I believe you've beaten yourself up more than I've wanted to beat you."

Justice acknowledged his words with a nod.

"It's difficult for me to acknowledge that I made mistakes with Lucía. I never saw the way she was treated by certain members of my household and when I did see it, I didn't react. I should have, and perhaps she wouldn't have felt the need to escape as she did."

"With all due respect, and I don't disagree with all that you said, but I don't think it would've changed the outcome. Lucía is stubborn and passionate about what she does, but she's also the most wonderful, loving, kind person I know."

The King cocked his head, a frown on his brow. "You want to marry my daughter?"

"Yes, I do. I love her more than anything in this world."

"Even any children you may have?"

The question stunned Reaper, but he replied with honesty because he knew that was what the King deserved. "No, it isn't the same. I'd always choose our children over anything, including Lucía because that's what a parent should do. I've been lucky enough to have a parent that chose me time and time again over everything else and that's what I'd want for my children. That said, I'd still die for her because she's my world."

Reaper didn't feel comfortable being so open about his emotions, but he needed to be transparent if he was to achieve his goal.

"I respect your honesty." The King stood and moved to the antique table where a crystal decanter was filled with amber liquid. He held the decanter up and Reaper nodded. Pouring them both a glass he handed Reaper his and took a sip as he walked to the window. "You are not the man I would have chosen for my daughter."

Reaper felt his gut twist and took a sip of the smooth brandy to ease the ache. "I know. I'm nobody. I have no title, no long, elaborate family history, and although I'm reasonably well off due to my job, I'm not rich like Lucía."

193

The King looked him over. "No you are not, but despite all that, my daughter loves you and you make her happy. I haven't failed to see the way she smiles these days or the light that surrounds her when you are together. You shine the spotlight on her and make her the sole focus of any room you are in, and that's what she deserves after so long in the shadow of her sister and I."

He thought his heart might beat out of his chest as the King approached him. Reaper stood face to face and toe to toe with the most powerful man in the country, and one of the most powerful in the world.

"If I grant you permission to marry my daughter, I need your word that when the time comes for my Maria to lead this great country, that Lucía will be by her side. She'll need her sister's guidance and counsel. They're close and I do not want that to change."

"You have my word."

"Then you have my blessing."

"Thank you, sir."

A slight dip of his head was the only response. "Now, what of your job?"

Reaper knew it had been too good to be true. "Lucía and I have discussed it and she wants to move to the UK and buy a property similar to what she has in Whitmore but near where I work. I know my job isn't normal and if she wants me to give it up I will, but she says she doesn't." Reaper was being polite, but the details were only between the two of them.

"I should hope not. The world needs men like you, and despite what happened, you're good at it. With Lucía wanting to pull back from her royal duties, will it remain safe for you to do what you do?"

"Yes, and we have measures in place to ensure our photo isn't plastered around the world and any jobs we do won't lead back to me. We're careful."

"You mean you don't leave witnesses?"

Reaper remained silent, not willing to discuss the details of Shadow with even the King.

The man held up his hand. "Enough said. As long as she's safe and you can both lead a life that will make you happy."

"I'll make her happy, sir. I promise."

"Then it's time for you to ask my daughter what she thinks, don't you agree?"

Reaper grinned, feeling like a boy about to ask his first crush on a date. Every day he woke feeling almost giddy with happiness that she loved him back and had forgiven him.

"Yes, sir."

"Juan will do when we're alone since we'll be family."

Reaper thrust out his hand to the King, who gripped it firmly. "Thank you, Juan."

Then he left, rushing to intercept Lucía before the Valentine's Ball began to raise money for Books for All.

Lucía looked down at the slip of paper that Justice had given her that morning as he had every day since the first of February. Each day had held a note telling her why he loved her and all the things he wanted to do with her in the future. Some had been so hot it was a wonder that the paper hadn't gone up in flames. Others were sweet plans or places he wanted to see with her.

She didn't think she could love him more but every day he proved to her that she was wrong. His being there for the Valentine's Ball, when she knew he hated to wear a suit and be around some of her family, was proof enough of his love for her.

Maria adored him and so did her mother. He and Lucas got on well too, but her father was still somewhat reserved and her aunt was openly disapproving. Somehow that didn't bother her as it would have in the past. Now she was at peace with who she was and her place in the world.

She may not be the centre of this world or this family, and she was okay with that because she was the centre of Justice's world.

He'd made her see her qualities and what she had to offer and not apologise for being herself and wanting things for herself.

As she ran her hands along the paper in her hand, she read the message asking her to meet him in the almond grove at noon again. She adored this time of year when the almond trees blossomed into creams and pale pinks, transforming the barren winter into the stunning beauty of spring.

This time always heralded a new start and was her favourite time of year to visit the gardens. Oh, she loved the height of summer, but this was special in a way she couldn't explain.

Turning the corner into the meadow that had been her safe place in this world, her breath caught. Her hand flew to her mouth at the sight of Justice on one knee, a tiny ring box in his hand.

Her steps slowed but as if by a magnet she continued, not knowing if she could trust this was real or a dream. "Justice?"

"Come here, my love."

Lucía quickened her pace toward the man who held her heart. When she was close enough, he took her hand in his and she could feel the tremble in this tough man's body as he swallowed steadying himself. "God, I didn't think I'd be so nervous."

Lucía smiled, her heart kicking in her chest with love for him.

"Lucía, I never wanted love. It was never in my plans to fall in love and give someone the power to hurt me. Then I met you and you made me see that it wasn't a choice. When two people who are destined to be together meet, the heart decides for you without consent or compassion for your plans. You make me a better man, a better friend, and I hope one day the best father. Most of all, I want the chance to make the best husband. Will you be my wife, for better or worse?"

Tears blurred her vision, and her smile was wide enough for the heavens to see. "Yes, I'd love to be your wife."

"Oh, thank God."

Justice took the ring from the box and with shaky fingers pushed the single solitaire over her knuckle. Standing, he took her in his arms and kissed her, as if his only purpose in life was to do so.

Life may not be simple for them, but it would always be worth it to feel like she did at that moment with the man she loved holding her and her future full of so much promise.

THIS MIGHT BE the happy ever after for Reaper and Lucía, but for a sneak peek of Bishop and Charlie's whirlwind story, read on.

SNEAK PEEK: STOLEN SALVATION

BLOOD BLOOMED ON HIS SHOULDER, AND SHE FELT NAUSEA STIR IN HER BELLY, but it was the look of utter shock and betrayal on his face that shredded her heart into tiny pieces. The only man she'd ever loved was shot at her own hand. Lowering her weapon, she fought the urge to go to him, to help him and beg him to forgive her, to listen to her reasons, but none of them mattered. That single shot had ended any chance she might have of a happy ever after with him. Hell, with anyone. Nobody compared to Noah Bishop, they never had. From the second they'd met years ago, it had been the two of them against the world.

But the world had won, tearing them apart and making a mockery of the vows they'd made to each other. To love, honour, and defend, in sickness and in health. How cruel that she was doing all those things as she watched him bleed, his wound allowing the blood to seep from him.

"Come, Lottie, it's time for us to leave."

Cocking her head to the powerful and deadly man behind her, she set her jaw to stop the snarl edging up her throat. He needed to believe she was who she said she was, or they'd both die.

"Coming, Armand." Her voice held an adoring quality, the false-ness obvious to her and anyone who knew her. But this man had more ego than anyone she'd ever met. It was what made him so dangerous. She had to stop him, but she'd never wanted it to go down this way. For her husband, the man she loved, to end up as collateral damage.

Shifting the white dress so it didn't get into the blood at her feet, she crouched as if picking up her designer clutch. Laying a hand on Noah's arm, she watched his eyes flicker open, pain from the earlier beating at the hands of Armand and his men already making him weak. "I'm so sorry."

A strong hand gripped her wrist and she blinked away tears. "Don't do this, Charlie."

Pain echoed through her heart, shattering her in a way she knew she'd never be whole again. "I'm sorry, I don't have a choice."

"We always have a choice."

His voice was laced with pain, gritty and weak and she knew he'd fall unconscious soon and she needed to be gone when he did. "You're wrong."

Ripping her arm from his grip, she hated that the last time he touched her would be etched on her soul with the betrayal in his eyes. His head fell back, and he looked away as if her face caused him pain and distaste.

As she straightened her back and walked away head held high, she knew that Noah would never know how hard this was for her or how her world shattered that night. He'd hate her but she'd saved him, and that was all that mattered.

BOOKS BY MADDIE WADE

FORTIS SECURITY

Healing Danger (Dane and Lauren)

Stolen Dreams (Nate and Skye)

Love Divided (Jace and Lucy)

Secret Redemption (Zack and Ava)

Broken Butterfly (Zin and Celeste)

Arctic Fire (Kanan and Roz)

Phoenix Rising (Daniel and Megan)

Nate & Skye Wedding Novella

Digital Desire (Will and Aubrey)

Paradise Ties: A Fortis Wedding Novella (Jace and Lucy & Dane and Lauren)

Wounded Hearts (Drew and Mara)

Scarred Sunrise (Smithy and Lizzie)

Zin and Celeste: A Fortis Family Christmas

Fortis Boxset 1 (Books 1-3)

Fortis Boxset 2 (Books 4-7.5

EIDOLON

Alex

Blake

Reid

Liam

Mitch

Gunner

Waggs

Jack

Lopez

Decker

ALLIANCE AGENCY SERIES (CO-WRITTEN WITH INDIA KELLS)

Deadly Alliance

Knight Watch

Hidden Obsession

Lethal Justice

Innocent Target

Power Play

RYOSHI DELTA (PART OF SUSAN STOKER'S POLICE AND FIRE: OPERATION ALPHA WORLD)

Condor's Vow

Sandstorm's Promise

Hawk's Honor

Omega's Oath

Lyric's Truth (coming soon)

SHADOW ELITE

Guarding Salvation

Innocent Salvation

Royal Salvation

Stolen Salvation

TIGHTROPE DUET

Tightrope One

Tightrope Two

ANGELS OF THE TRIAD

01 Sariel

OTHER WORLDS

Keeping Her Secrets *Suspenseful Seduction World* (Samantha A. Cole's World)

Finding English P*olice and Fire: Operation Alpha* (Susan Stoker's world)

About the Author

Contact Me

If stalking an author is your thing and I sure hope it is then here are the links to my social media pages.

If you prefer your stalking to be more intimate, then my group Maddie's Minxes will welcome you with open arms.

General Email: info.maddiewade@gmail.com
Email: maddie@maddiewadeauthor.co.uk
Website: http://www.maddiewadeauthor.co.uk
Facebook page: https://www.facebook.com/maddieuk/
Facebook group: https://www.facebook.com/groups/546325035557882/
Amazon Author page: amazon.com/author/maddiewadeGoodreads: https://www.goodreads.com/author/show/14854265.Maddie_Wade
Bookbub: https://partners.bookbub.com/authors/3711690/edit
Twitter: @mwadeauthor
Pinterest: @maddie_wade
Instagram: Maddie Author

WANT A FREE SHORT STORY?

Sign up for Maddie's Newsletter using the link below and receive a free copy of the short story, Fortis: Where it all Began.

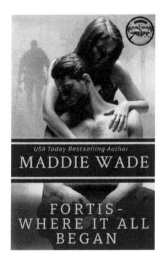

When hard-nosed SAS operator, Zack Cunningham is forced to work a mission with the fiery daughter of the American General, sparks fly. As those heated looks turn into scorching hot stolen kisses, a forbidden love affair begins that neither had expected.

Just as life is looking perfect disaster strikes and Ava Drake is left wondering if she will ever see the man she loves again.

https://dl.bookfunnel.com/cyrjtv3tta

Printed in Great Britain
by Amazon

13186297R00125